A DRAWING OF MURDER
A SEABREEZE BOOKSHOP COZY MYSTERY BOOK 9

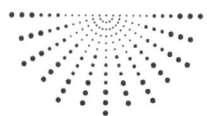

PENNY BROOKE

Copyright © 2023 by Penny Brooke

All rights reserved.

No part of this book may be reproduced in any form or by any electronic or mechanical means, including information storage and retrieval systems, without written permission from the author, except for the use of brief quotations in a book review.

This is a work of fiction. Names, places, characters, and incidents are either the product of the author's imagination or are used fictitiously, and any resemblance to any actual persons, living or dead, organizations, events or locales is entirely coincidental.

CHAPTER ONE

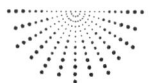

"I've been in the mood for pasta. Could you hold these while I browse?" Whitney Ackerman set a pile of cookbooks on the counter, then wandered toward the new-releases table. Her shoes—honest-to-goodness Louboutins—made soft clicks on the hardwood as she walked.

I gazed at the book jutting at an angle off the top of her pile. "Don't you even think of not inviting me if you decide to make this sausage-tortellini on the cover," I told her with a smile.

I was a fan of Whitney, and it wasn't just because the willowy middle-aged blonde was a bookseller's dream. In Whitney's privileged world, why would you google recipes for pasta primavera when you could buy five shiny hardback cookbooks? With full-color photos!

Ideas from top chefs and authentic recipes from Italian families for whom the perfect mingling of ingredients was a way of life.

While independent bookstores were beloved institutions to those who fed their souls within our walls, the financial end of things could be challenging at best. I did adore the customers who came in to only browse, touching one book and then another like a treasure until they could save enough to go home with the latest Kristin Hannah. But it was the Whitneys in our town who made that possible for the readers of Somerset Harbor, Massachusetts.

And beyond that, she was a friend. I loved the way that Whitney always brought the party when she came into the store. She could describe the latest meeting of the recreation board in such a way that more than once, the two of us had laughed until we cried. The stories seemed to simply spill out of her mouth.

And today I was prepared with some stories of my own, having just returned from a long overdue vacation. I had already filled her in on the highlights from Hawaii.

"Oh!" My eyes grew wide. "And I forgot to tell you that when I got to the hotel and opened up my luggage, it did not belong to me!" I said. "Somebody had a suitcase identical to mine, but they were much less fun. Like, their idea of a beach book was—you will not believe it—*The Secret Wondrous World of Microorganisms!*"

That horrific fact earned only a slight smile from my friend. "Well, that's just sad for them," she said.

She picked up a book as I told her how I'd been reunited quickly with my luggage—and my carefully selected thrillers.

Something was very off about my friend today. Whitney never was this quiet.

"Everything okay?" I asked, reading a recipe for pesto chicken pasta I might fix for myself soon.

She reached down to pet Gatsby, golden retriever extraordinaire and the official greeter of the Seabreeze Bookshop. "Oh, I'm getting by," she said, letting out a sigh. "But what a scary thought—that just four days from now, all of them will be here, descending on the house. The Ackermans in all their glory—all forty-two of them." She winced.

For months she'd been describing—comically of course—her efforts to whip the house into shape for the annual reunion of the clan, who would be coming in from across New England.

And that must have been a job. I had been to Whitney's house, which was gorgeous but a mess. She would rather read, create homemade soaps, or volunteer at the food pantry than pay attention to her house. "Life is just too short to sort through all those piles of dusty stuff," she had told me once, waving a manicured hand dismissively through the air.

I might have even said that Whitney was a bit of a hoarder. The house was clean enough—she had maid service once a week—but the boxes and the piles seemed to have taken over every nook and corner. Had she never heard of throwing stuff away?

I had seen it all up close since Whitney had been generous enough to invite me for dinner several times, as some customers will do. In their minds, they're saving me from one more single-woman's dinner of cereal, a bagel, or something quick and sad. (I, in fact, make an awesome burgundy beef stew and have perfected the art of freezing simple comfort foods in small convenient batches.)

I thought now about the bulging bags and boxes strewn across the guest beds and crammed into the closets where her guests would need to hang their clothes. Three of the Ackermans, I knew, would be staying at her home, while she had reserved hotel rooms for the others.

But hopefully, I thought, all of that was cleared by now. And it was odd to see a project that could put a dent in the boundless energy and fun that was Whitney Ackerman. Just the week before, she'd been laughing at how many dirty towels she'd unearthed from underneath the bed and piles of shoes in her oldest daughter Candace's bedroom. "And this whole time I'd been afraid some towel-eating gremlin had been set loose in the house," she had told me with a wicked sparkle in her eye. "I was thinking one day soon I'd have to skip my showers—or just hop out and drip dry."

Gatsby's joyful yips signaled the entrance of Elizabeth, my best friend and co-worker, who had been working in the back. "Whitney!" She smiled from ear to ear. "Tell me a story; make me laugh. It's been that kind of day."

But Whitney only nodded and let out a sigh. "You can say that again—a trial of a day."

Elizabeth tilted her head, concerned, putting down a pile of books. "Well, your big weekend is getting close. How are the girls?" she asked.

"Well, Candace is back at home, you know, hoping to find a job. Although for now she's volunteered to bunk in with her sister—to make room for her Uncle Matt while he's here in town. It was the thing to do, of course, after all that Matt has done for us. But that meant quite the job for Candace, cleaning up her space for him. She takes after me, I guess. Neatness, I'm afraid, is not a virtue that either I or Candace hold close to our heart."

She sank down into a reading chair we kept close to the counter.

Whitney had lost her husband, David, to a heart attack six years before, and his three brothers had stepped in to fill the void in the lives of her girls. That had been especially true for Matt, to whom David had been closest. The two of them had been partners in a chain of stores that was now the market leader in upscale sporting goods in thirty states and growing,

"In fact, Matt's already here," reported Whitney. "To get those rental tables set up and to clear some heavy junk that's collected by the pool. And the other girls are fine. Kate finished up at Amherst back in June, so all three of them are home, and Laila's doing well. Never any drama with our last one." She gave us a small grin. "Third time's the charm, I guess."

Candace, I understood, had been the main challenge for her mother through the years. Legend had it that she'd turned the family's pool bright purple and filled it with rubber ducks the night her mother hosted a reception for the governor, in town to campaign for re-election.

Candace was now twenty-six, Kate was twenty-one, and Laila was sixteen. They all were pretty blondes, and the oldest two were almost identical except that Kate's long hair fell in curls while Candace's was sleek and straight.

As if on cue, Candace strode in with two coffees from Evan's on the corner. "With a shot of vanilla," she said to her mother, handing her a coffee. Then she smiled at me. "Hello, Ms. Collier!" She burst into laughter as Gatsby ran around in happy circles before covering her hand with doggy kisses. "Your dog remembers me!"

"Oh, Gatsby is a big fan of all the pretty girls," I said. "It's good to see you, Candace. Welcome home." Candace occasionally popped into the store to browse through the graphic novels when she was in town for a visit. Since her graduation from UMass, she had found it difficult to hold down a job, according to her mother. Accustomed as she was to the easy life afforded by her family's wealth, she'd been taken by surprise by the world of work, where you could not just take a "me day" because it looked like rain—or abandon an assignment that failed to "stimulate one's creativity."

But I was rooting for her. More naïve than entitled, Candace had an open heart and giving spirit.

Quiet as usual, the youngest sister, Laila, had trailed in behind Candace, a coffee in her hand and her ever-present sketch pad tucked beneath her arm. She settled at a table and started drawing right away with her features mostly shrouded by her long blonde hair. "How are you, Ms. Collier?" she greeted me politely.

"Hey, Laila. Doing great." Then I thought of something. "Oh, Whitney! I almost forgot." I pulled a book from beneath the counter and held it up for her. "I took the liberty last month of putting this on order. For your presidential project." Whitney was systematically making her way through books about each president in order, having made it by that point to Millard Fillmore. This idea of hers had been fun for me as well as I tried to curate a variety of reading for my best customer, mixing in some special-focus books along with the more typical biography formats. The one I held in my hand was centered around a large stash of letters, thought to have been lost or destroyed, between the president and Dorothea Dix, a crusader for the humane treatment of the mentally ill.

Across the room, Elizabeth helped two women in the travel section. As they moved on to browse, they paused for a moment to watch Laila sketch.

Whitney moved closer to the counter to glance briefly at the book. "That looks great," she said, but her eyes soon strayed away as she checked her phone. Normally, the unveiling of a new presidential book, the beginning of a new era in politics as it were, was cause for celebration.

I noticed she looked pale as she handed me the last of her book selections, and her hand was trembling as she pulled her Mastercard out of her wallet. Candace added *Ninth House* to the pile, and Laila shyly handed me a portrait of Gatsby, his head tilted to one side as he eagerly watched the happenings around him. She had captured perfectly his look of anticipation, as if he was hoping somebody would step into the picture, grab the rope toy near his paw, and start a game of tug-of-war.

"This is amazing, Laila. This could be a photograph," I said.

She shrugged, but her smile showed that she was pleased with my reaction.

When they were gone, I taped the portrait to the front of the desk for customers to see. Then I went to the tea station in the corner and made myself a cup. I was suddenly engulfed by a sense of unease. "Whitney's not herself," I said. "Elizabeth, I'm worried. Something just seems off."

"I get what you mean. She was just so…serious, which is not like Whitney," Elizabeth agreed. "And she was so quiet too—at least by Whitney standards."

Quiet was a thing Whitney didn't do. I was amazed sometimes—and a little mortified—by the way she overshared to strangers in the store—about her dating drama, problems with indigestion, almost anything at all.

I bent down to pick up my cat Beasley, who had pressed his cold nose against my ankle, looking for attention—or maybe a cat treat.

"I have, like, these warning bells going off inside my gut," I told Elizabeth. And very, very rarely did my feelings steer me wrong when it came to the regulars who came into the store. While helping my customers discover fabulous new things to read, I had learned to read my customers.

Thoughtfully, Elizabeth ran a hand through her long hair. "Well, that isn't good. A feeling of foreboding, and just as Whitney gets to unlucky number thirteen—you know, with Millard Fillmore."

"Unlucky! Millard Fillmore!" called out our parrot, Zeke, startling a man who had settled in the Book Nook with a hardback.

Elizabeth had recently become enamored with a popular new book on "superstitions and why practical-minded people should listen to their truths."

In my head, I rolled my eyes; thirteen was just a *number*. I had too much to do on any given day to be intimidated by a one followed by a three.

But four days later, I had to wonder if Elizabeth was right. That was when my buddy Andy came into the store near closing, a grim look on his face. I had already started turning out the lights, and everyone had gone by then.

"Andy, what has happened?" I asked him, alarmed.

Because he was a detective, the first thing that popped into my head was a plea to the universe: *Please don't let someone be dead.* That might seem alarmist, but for an upscale tourist area, we seemed to have way more than our fair share of murders. In fact, I hardly ever reached for a mystery anymore; they hit too close to home.

Andy placed a hand on his ample stomach and rubbed the other hand over his receding hairline. "I knew you'd want to know, being close to Whitney."

Luckily, I was near the Book Nook, where I could sink into a chair. I didn't trust my legs to hold me up for one more second. "Andy! What do you mean?"

Being a smart dog who could always read the room, Gatsby let out a mournful howl.

"Physically, she's fine," Andy told me gently, "but I'm afraid that…well, Candace's body was discovered about three o'clock this afternoon."

I let out a gasp. "*What?* But, Andy…*why?* I don't understand."

"She was stabbed out in the pool house of the family home. Which is where I've just come from. They were having some reunion-type of thing, it seemed. Lots of family around."

Stabbed? It all seemed unreal.

"Do you know who did it?" I asked him.

"They're still questioning the people over at the house. There were quite a lot of them, and no suspects have emerged—but it's still early in the process. In fact, I need to get on back there now and help. But let me drive you home. You have had a shock."

All I could do was nod and go through the motions of closing up the store.

"Thank you, Andy. Yes."

CHAPTER TWO

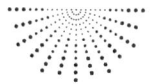

The next day I woke up numb.

Andy had given me the basics, but there were so many questions and not a lot of answers. Most of the reunion group had gotten into town and were gathered on the pool deck when they found…well, I couldn't think about it.

Candace had apparently gone into the pool house to get more drinks from the fridge. When she did not return—and the drink table had been emptied of chardonnay and soda—her three uncles had gone in to check and found her with a knife thrust into her chest. The paramedics had been called, but it was too late. They estimated Candace had died fairly quickly after the attack.

Andy said the cops were hopeful the knife could

provide some clues—fingerprints, perhaps. "The plan is to get prints from everybody who was on the scene," he said. "Then if we can lift some prints from the weapon, we'll hope for a match."

"Surely they don't think it was someone from the family?" I had asked.

He had stared straight ahead as he drove me home. "I'm afraid for now that is the theory," he told me. "It just makes more sense. It seems unlikely some intruder could have snuck into the pool house with all those people there. The area is gated with the house on one side and the street close on the other."

"But it could have happened, right? That it was a stranger?" Because if it was someone from the family who had murdered Candace, that would be a whole new layer of horrific for Whitney to take in.

"It's not impossible," said Andy with a shrug as he braked for a light. "Wealth can be a reason people target homes, but one would have to think someone from the outside would have picked a time when three or four of the Ackermans were there and not forty-two of them."

"That makes sense," I said.

But nothing made sense, really. This was supposed to be the year Candace got her act together, maybe found her passion…or even fell in love! All of the exhilarating things a girl does in her twenties. She was supposed to spend the weekend dunking cousins in the pool and drinking too much wine and telling family tales.

Until someone decided no.

I glanced at the clock—six thirty on the dot—but I had no desire to get out of bed.

And yet even so, three pairs of eyes were pinned on me just inches from my pillow. One member of the household might have wanted to hide beneath the sheets, but the other family members were eager for their breakfast.

Plus, there was a store to run, so I forced myself out of bed to begin the day.

Later at the bookshop, I tried to lose myself in my current project of updating the store's website and social media. I looked through some of the photos I had picked to possibly be placed at the top of the home page. One showed our high-end book bags hanging up behind the beach-reads table, a pair of Ray-Bans posed playfully on top of a paperback. In another photo, there were my two cats peeking out of a half-empty box of new books. Choosing photographs was supposed to be the fun part, but my heart wasn't in it.

Thankfully, there was the distraction of lots of traffic in the store. When there was major news in town

—and a murder qualified, of course—people in Somerset Harbor liked to be out and about, trading information. I found a lot of comfort in the company of others who felt the same devastation that I did, a sinking kind of feeling that made it hard sometimes to breathe.

And I liked to think I helped them too by recommending books they could escape into for a little while at least. During times of tragedy, the bookshop felt especially important with its neatly ordered worlds of fiction available to all when the real world was too much.

About three, we hit a lull, and I told Elizabeth I felt compelled to go to Whitney. "She's got family around—a lot of family—but maybe it would help to…oh, I don't know, just be there for her?" I asked. I had been looking through some templates for the website, but almost any task I did seemed so unimportant compared to Whitney's loss.

"I think that would be nice." Elizabeth gave me a small nod.

Our new part-timer Beth was set to show up in thirty minutes, so I headed out.

The sun was shining into my car on the short drive over. It reflected off the white pines and made sparkles on the water as I made my way past the beach. The perfect breeze and white light seemed out of sync with the sense of anguish that settled over the town.

Whitney's circular driveway was filled with cars, and they were lined up as well in front of her massive white brick house with its immaculately manicured green lawn. The Ackermans, I was sure, had come into town in a mood to celebrate. Now I could feel the distress almost shouting from behind the red double doors.

Whitney's side of the family, I supposed, had arrived to mourn as well, making for an even fuller house.

I could see remnants of crime-scene tape as I moved down the sidewalk while blue and white balloons floated sadly from the mailbox. Then, quietly, I knocked, and the door was answered by a woman who looked a lot like Whitney, except her face was a little fuller and she was on the shorter side.

"I am a friend of Whitney's," I told her quietly. "Is she up for company? Or would the family prefer to have… you know, some time?"

Should I have brought a dish, or should I have even come? Was I intruding here? Who knew what was right and wrong in these kinds of situations?

She smoothed down the skirt of her pale-green cotton dress. "Oh, come on in. I'm Jean, Whitney's sister from Vermont."

"I'm Rue," I said as Whitney spotted me from across

the room, and I made my way to her with open arms. She seemed to have aged ten years in the few days since I'd seen her.

"Oh, your precious girl," I said, giving her a hug.

I could see the middle daughter, Kate, staring blankly out a window in a far corner of the room. She was keeping to herself as the relatives murmured quietly in groups of twos or threes. Some of them were bunched around a table in the dining room across the hall. Big casserole dishes filled with food were spread across the table amid empty plates and glasses.

"And Kate and Laila, Whitney! How will they even bear it?" Tears pricked at my eyes.

"Kate has barely said a word to anybody since it happened," Whitney told me quietly. "She's been at odds with Candace since Candace came back home." She dabbed at her eye with a tissue. "Just sister stuff, I guess. But it makes it extra hard that stupid fate had to take her sister now—before they could make things right."

Had it been jealousy, I wondered, on the part of Candace? While the oldest daughter struggled, Kate made life seem easy. She had breezed through with top grades and a ton of friends while volunteering at a senior center and breaking records for her college softball team. Now, after her graduation with a marketing degree, I understood that Kate was weighing several offers from prestigious companies. Not that any of those things could ease her heartache now.

"Do you have *any idea* who would have...?" I let my voice trail away. I was there to comfort and not to voice my own questions and distress.

Whitney shook her head. "It just seems impossible that anyone would...*why would they do it, Rue?* I just keep thinking, *Why?*"

She was looking weak, so I led her to a seat, and two teenage girls scooted over to make some room for us on the blue plush couch.

"My friend, Rue," she told them by way of introduction, and they looked up from their phones to nod solemnly at me.

"So sorry for your loss," I said just as Jean appeared with a glass of water for her sister.

Three middle-aged men across the room were staring at the floor, their arms folded across their chests. Their poses were identical, but the tallest one seemed to glare at the floor as if the polished hardwood and the fine Persian rug had been the ones to kill his family member. Something about the man's expression gave me chills, heightening the feeling of foreboding that had stuck with me since Whitney's last visit to the store.

"Candace's uncles," Jean explained when she saw me looking. "We call them the Jokers Three but just for fun, of course. There used to be four of them—the brothers—when Whitney's David was alive."

Sensing Whitney was exhausted, I squeezed her hand and told her to call me anytime as I stood to go. "I'll check in with you soon," I said.

I headed to the door, and Jean walked part of the way with me, glancing at the uncles. "It was those three who found her," she told me in a whisper. "And ever since they saw…what they saw, they've barely moved or said a word. Understandable, of course, but every now and then, I'll shove some water bottles at them and hold my ground until they drink. The Ackermans, you know, tend to get a little dizzy when they forget to drink their water; hydration is important."

It must run in the family, that tendency to overshare.

She gave me a small smile. "It's nice to know my sister has dear friends close by," she said. "I worry about Whitney, and I sensed some trouble with her, even before I got the news that we had lost our girl. Something was eating at her last week; there was something on her mind." She paused. "A sister knows these things."

"She seemed a little quiet the last time I saw her too."

"But she refused to talk about it, which is not the way with us," Jean told me with a frown. "We always talk things out."

Someone called her from the kitchen, and I moved to

a long table near the entrance, where some had lit candles and lined up photographs of Candace: sitting on the beach, laughing with her family, waving from the driver's seat of her red Porsche.

Just beyond the table was a small room where I could see Laila sketching with her back to me; a bunch of colored pencils were fanned out beside her, waiting. I thought of going to her, but I sensed her sketch pad was the kind of balm reading was for me.

I was close enough, however, to see the figure of a young man she had almost finished drawing. The man's eyes were closed as he seemed to float beneath jagged waves of bluish green. The bold forceful strokes gave the impression that the pool—the sea?—was angry. And prominent in the drawing was a hand that held the young man beneath the surface, even as his arm reached toward the pale-yellow light.

Then my eyes moved to the borders, where Laila had added thumbnail sketches of a skull, a tombstone, bloody teardrops, and faces wracked with grief.

So much darkness in this house, I thought as my chest went cold. Was this just an artistic way for Laila to express her grief for her sister? Or was this a memory that might explain why someone had gone after Candace?

Desperate for some fresh air, I quietly slipped out.

CHAPTER THREE

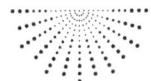

Two nights later, Andy stared into the dying sun as he nursed a glass of whiskey on my porch. "This investigation is a challenge, makes me feel my age," he said.

Beasley nuzzled closer in his lap, as if to assure him it would be okay.

Andy had explained that on one hand, it was good to have "known people" who had been present at a murder scene—with both opportunity and access to the victim. But in the case of the Ackermans, there had been forty-two. Forty-two intensive interviews. Forty-two background checks. Forty-two mostly boisterous men and women with voices that carried across the room, talking over one another at the scene. And that was just the family of the late David Ackerman; the next day Whitney's sister and her sons had rushed into town to join the mourners. "Of course, we've talked to them as well to see what they might know," said Andy.

I winced sympathetically. "Anyone stand out?" I stroked the soft white fur of Ollie, the smallest of the cats. Andy and I were like mirror images in the twilight, each with a cat companion and a half-full glass of Maker's Mark while Gatsby dozed blissfully between us.

Andy raised an eyebrow at my question and took a sip of whiskey while I waited for an answer—or any kind of hint. It had become our routine when a tragic killing rocked our town, something that happened frequently enough it had begun to worry those who made their living in the restaurants and hotels. Or anybody else who depended on the tourists, which was almost all of us in our little haven near Cape Cod. But despite our worries, Somerset Harbor had retained its status as a sun-kissed jewel for tourists, who continued to pour in for the season. And they were right to do so; they were absolutely safe. There had, after all, never been a stranger-on-stranger murder in our town, just tragic personal situations that had horrific ends.

Andy, stubborn as he was, still held his tongue, so I tried another question that had been on my mind. "What's the story with the uncles?"

If the horrid theory held—that someone in the

family had killed Candace—would the cops be looking hard at the "Jokers Three," who had, after all, been the ones to find the body?

Andy gave me a rueful smile as he sipped his drink. "I cannot discuss this, Rue, which I believe you know."

I cocked my head at him. "Beasley and Ollie can keep secrets, and Gatsby's off in Dreamland." Which anyone could tell by the explosive snores.

My comments were met with silence.

I took another sip. "Make sure you offer water to the uncles in future interviews. If they neglect their water—which they are prone to do—they tend to start feeling dizzy, which I imagine would result in them giving less information to the cops."

Andy frowned. "Okay. Well, then…thanks?" He paused for a moment. "You've been at Whitney's, then, I take it." There was a warning in his voice mixed in with frustration. Andy understood that when I cared about a topic, I was the kind to go all in and dig for information. And when the subject was a murder, the cop part of Andy worried. (He had retired from the force by then to start his own investigative firm. But we had a small police department, and the chief still called him in when needed.)

Anytime I took an interest in a case, I sensed Andy was afraid I would find myself in the crosshairs of some killer—which was just absurd. It was true that I on occasion got involved with the victims' families. Because of course I did if they were friends of mine. And the town was small enough that if you ran a business, you got to know a good percentage of the people here. In the case of the Seabreeze Bookshop, you got to know them *very well* if they were regulars and your discussions on the books they liked ran deep.

And now, how could I stay uninvolved when my heart was breaking for Whitney and her girls? Already I was hearing things—and seeing things—the cops should know. If they didn't know already.

I ran a finger softly from the top of Ollie's head to the middle of his back. "Have the cops made a connection between the killing and…some kind of drowning?"

Andy's eyes grew wide. "What on earth do you mean?"

I shrugged. "Oh, it's probably not related. Or for all I know, it never even happened." I only knew the image had disturbed me. I could still see the raised hand as the man tried to save himself, the tears and anguished faces around the border of the art.

"Hey, Andy, just one question. What did Laila have to say? About who could have hurt her sister?"

Andy was watching me, still startled by the mention of a drowning. "She barely said a word."

"Oh, yes. She's a quiet one, but sometimes those are the types who see and know the most." I paused. "For Laila, it's her art that helps her express her feelings. She pours it out onto the page." I told him what I'd seen, and he nodded, taking it all in.

"Watch the sketch pad, Andy." I leaned back in my chair. "It might have a lot to say."

"As far as any kind of drowning," Andy said, "nothing comes to mind right off the cuff with connections to the family. But first thing in the morning, I'll be looking into that." He took a slow sip of his drink, then he shook his head. "They lost David way too young, and now Candace has been taken from the family as well. This one's a heartbreaker."

We each fell into our own thoughts as the night grew even darker, and I found myself wondering again what had been going on with Whitney the week before the murder.

"I know one of David's brothers—Matt, I think it was—got here early in the week to help get things set up," I said. "Were there any others who came in early too?" Maybe something had gone on with the first arrivals that had ended with that knife. It seemed unlikely to me, but then again, so did the murder.

"Matt's been at the house since last Sunday. Most of the others got there the same day as the murder. A few came the day before." Andy paused to sip his drink. "As long as I have done this, it still does something to me, that look of utter devastation on the faces of the families." He closed his eyes, lost in thought. "Matt runs the family business, a substantial operation, and that gave us a good witness with a head for detail. Very, very helpful. He was able to give us a good idea of when Candace left the pool deck to grab the extra drinks, whom she spoke with the most, and so on. Bright fellow—very tall—that you might have noticed at the house."

Tall. So Matt had been the man who had given me the creeps. Whose furious expression had amped up my sense of dread—like there was some horror still to come.

But of course the man was angry. Because Matt was the uncle who had stepped up the most to be a father figure to the girls, to let Whitney lean on him during the harder years with Candace. For him, it must have been like walking in to find a daughter on that pool-house floor.

Then Andy stood to go. He was watching me intently. "You seem to have a radar on the family, Rue. Have you heard anything at all about a prep kit with food supplies—flashlights and blankets and the like?"

I looked at him, startled. "Like things people get

together in case of World War Three? Or an asteroid? Zombie apocalypse?"

Andy rubbed his chin. "Except a high-end version. With a tent and solar panels for technical devices and assorted other stuff." He paused to clear his throat. "Also very useful if someone were to wish…to up and disappear. To be gone for quite a while."

"That never came up, no." My mind was kind of blown. "Andy, what is going on?"

But he simply shook his head. Looking beyond exhausted, he gently set down Beasley. "Good night, little man." Then he turned to me. "I would appreciate it if you'd keep me informed."

He headed down the steps and turned around when he reached the yard. "In the meantime, Rue, this conversation never happened. I never said a word."

CHAPTER FOUR

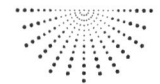

After the services for Candace at a packed Somerset Harbor Presbyterian, all of us in town tried to resume our normal schedules. But a heaviness had woven itself into all our activities, and it held on fast.

Seated at my desk, I typed a few sentences of a blog post to be added to the new site when we got it up. *Characters Most Likely to Be My BFFs if They Were Only Real.* But it seemed impossible almost to plan some bookish party on the beach with Elizabeth Bennet and Jo March when some killer was still out there. Maybe they were sitting down at that very moment to enjoy some crab cakes. Or they might be waiting to catch the perfect wave while Whitney and her girls would be forever changed. Maybe they were sitting on Whitney's couch right now or rifling through her fridge.

Or maybe they were just about to make their escape into oblivion, given Andy's odd remark about some lavish prep kit. Something must be done—and fast. If what he'd hinted at had merit, they'd have the supplies to hide out somewhere remote until the investigation stalled. And after that? A new life somewhere else? If that plot were in a book, I'd call the whole thing "outlandish."

I spun a pen in an idle circle as I thought. All that preparation would mean the murder had been planned as opposed to someone snapping. Which was incomprehensible to me.

I ran my hand through my hair and leaned back in my desk chair. How to tell which member of a big family group might be taking the final steps right now to—poof—disappear from their current life?

Then it came to me. One of my customers, a millionaire named Baxter Ridley, was a proud and avid prepper. Having made a fortune in pharmaceuticals, he was the kind of guy who could afford to have anything he wanted. And what Baxter wanted was a plan of escape.

"Something's going to get us," he had once confided to me. "Something cataclysmic with the weather, a government collapse."

To keep him and his family safe, he had a helicopter at the ready at all times. His "doomsday home" was stocked and ready somewhere across the ocean. Three bags of supplies were packed with everything he needed to keep living the high life, out of the reach of whatever horror fate might throw at the world.

He had invited me to meetings of his "survivor group," which I had declined. But I was aware that he and a group of rich-retiree prepper guys liked to hang out quite a lot on the west side of the beach, close to Pete's Fish and Chips. I got the idea that for most of the men, dabbling in prepping was a hobby, like smoking fine cigars and collecting classic cars.

These hangouts were no secret. There were signs all over town. *Be Ready When It Comes! Prepping Tips for All!* The group seemed to meet a lot—every other afternoon, in fact—at the cocktail hour. These men, after all, didn't have to punch a clock.

It could well be, I decided, that any Ackerman with a mind to escape might have seen the signs, and all of them had stayed in town to attend the service. Who was to say they might not drop in at a meeting to pick up some tips on disappearing? It would certainly be worth a stroll on the beach in that direction when the sun began to set. If nothing else, I'd have the chance to walk off some of my anxiety.

When I got off at five, I changed into the sneakers I kept in my office. Then I grabbed the leash and set off for the beach with a gleeful Gatsby. It was a bit of a walk to Pete's Fish and Chips, but the exercise felt good, and the springtime weather was like an invitation to linger out of doors. A chamber-of-commerce kind of day, for sure.

When we got to the west side, there was Baxter, sure enough, with three other men. They were lounging in their beach chairs with cocktails in their hands, looking none too worried about the end of the world. With his gray hair flying in the wind, he gave me a lazy wave, and Gatsby barked hello. The sun was down by then, but some light was coming from the full moon as well as from the beachside patio at Pete's.

I didn't know the others, but I'd seen them around. Which meant no Ackermans had joined the group today. Oh well. It had been a long shot, and I could always try again.

The exercise felt good, and Gatsby showed no signs of tiring, so we walked a little further. Until just minutes later I was stopped in my tracks by a familiar flash of blonde and a familiar gait. *Kate Ackerman.* It was Kate, walking at the spot where the surf splashed up to the middle of her calves.

This part of the beach was the furthest from her

house and with fewer hangouts. Interesting that she had chosen to walk here. Perhaps to be alone?

Wanting to watch her for a while in silence, I distracted Gatsby with some treats. Otherwise, the dog would be going mad with joy, barking his head off at the sight of Kate, who came into the store a lot for dystopian and fantasy and to smell the scented candles.

I watched as she moved further from the water and sat with her back to me, drawing something in the sand with a shell. Then she pulled her knees up, rested her head on the top of them, and wept.

Gatsby settled gently at my feet and waited quietly, seeming to understand his friend needed space.

When she had moved on, I waited a few minutes. Then I moved to the spot where she had drawn a large heart in the sand.

And there was a note she had carved beside it.

I am so sorry, Candace.

It wasn't long before the waves had washed the words away, and I got up and headed back, walking past the spot where Baxter and his buddies had packed up and left.

Kate's sobs still rang in my ear, and I was shaking as the weather seemed to change. Suddenly, the spring wind had taken on a chill.

CHAPTER FIVE

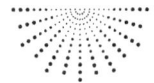

The next day I shelved some new arrivals while my mind spun around in circles. Was the death that had rocked our town simpler than it seemed, perhaps a robbery gone bad? Or could it be mixed up with a half-forgotten drowning somewhere in the past? Could it have been a long-planned murder by a family member who had already orchestrated a plan to disappear? Perhaps the seemingly too-perfect middle sister? Surely, not that last one. I brushed away the thought.

I'd put in a call to Baxter to ask—very casually, of course—how things were going with his group and if I'd be the only woman if I chanced to stop by. He hadn't called me back, but if he dropped Kate's name, my heart might just explode.

I shelved five of the latest Ruth Ware title and set aside some other copies within easy reach; those books would go quickly. My mind wandered to Candace and how happy she had seemed the last time I saw her. Being back with family would have done her good...except that being with her family seemed to have been her end. I paused in my work to close my eyes and take a cleansing breath.

"Um, excuse me? Ms. Collier? Hello!"

With Candace on my mind, I was startled to look up and see... Oh! Was that a ghost?

But no. It was Kate, of course, who could be her sister's twin.

I pressed my hand to my chest. "Kate! How in the world are you?" I gently touched her arm. "You and your mom and Laila, you have all been on my mind."

She gave me a sad smile, and her eyes were red and puffy as Ollie nosed her ankle.

She reached down to pick him up after setting a small pile of books on a nearby table. "I guess we're hanging in there. And I've found some books that I hope will help, although who am I kidding, right? There is no help for this—unless you have a time machine for sale. Because that's what I want—to go back to last week and lock the pool-house door. Or burn the whole thing down. To somehow stop what happened."

"And your mom? How is she?" I headed to the corner and fixed her a cup of rosehip tea, which I'd been told was good for stress. Then I led her to the Book Nook with its comfy chairs.

"Well, honestly, I came here for more than the books." She gazed at me shyly. "I was hoping you'd be here and that maybe you could help my mother. She thinks a lot of you."

"Anything at all I can do to help, you just give me the word."

"Well, you see, I'm really worried. I get that people grieve in all kinds of different ways, but my mother, she is…" There was a long pause. "All day and all night, she's cleaning up the house."

I was struck silent for a moment. "Oh. Well, that is…"

"So not her."

"Of course, if it brings her comfort…"

"I don't think it does. Because she is miserable, Ms. Collier, sobbing as she works. Emptying and sorting through one pile after another. One box and then the next one." She gave me a desperate look. "And that junk's been there *for years.* And she never ever cared."

We sat in silence for a moment as Beasley settled in on top of one of my black pumps to snooze.

Then Kate spoke again. "One of my aunts had this idea, to set up a scholarship as a way to honor Candace.

Because my sister would have liked that, for us to channel all the things we're feeling into something good, helping some young girl get ahead in life."

"I think that's lovely, Kate."

"That's who Candace was—the unselfish sister. I know she had her problems, but Candace was the sister who would never be a hater and fly off the handle and then...oh, just never mind." Kate paused to close her eyes and breathe. "I think Candace would have wanted us to help other girls."

My heart seemed to stop. "There were three unselfish sisters in your house," I said, "and you can't tell me any different."

Kate was breathing hard, but she got herself together. "So, I was kind of thinking you could maybe pop over to the house sometime? And try to...*refocus* mom on this scholarship idea. Maybe that would help."

"Should I stop by after work tonight? Or is there still family in town?"

"Only Uncle Matt and my Aunt Jean, which is nice." She sighed. "The family means well, but it's nice to have our space. So, yeah. If you could stop by after work, I think that would be great."

"Well, then, that will be our plan. And you're a good daughter, Kate, to come to me like this to try to help your mother." I put my hand on her knee. "It must be such a comfort for our Whitney to have you and Laila close."

A shadow crossed her face. "Will you promise me, Ms. Collier, you'll look after Mom and Laila? Because, well, some of my job offers are…you know, not so close."

I thought of her presence on the beach, just down from Baxter's group. And I thought of Andy's words: *If someone were to wish to up and disappear.*

But I squeezed her hand. She needed reassurance, not some suspicious bookstore sleuth.

"Well, hopefully, some intelligent employer not too far away will see what you have to offer. But, in any case, of course. I'll be there for them. As will lots of other people." I gave her a wink. "You know how we are in Somerset. Too much in people's business. But in the end, that's good, because no one is alone."

CHAPTER SIX

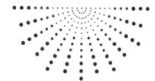

*L*ate that afternoon, I rang the bell at Whitney's. That set off a series of melodies and regal chimes that made me feel I had arrived at some grand cathedral.

As I began to wonder if anyone was home, I adjusted the foil-wrapped dish in my hands. (I had stopped on my way to pick up some lasagna. Since—in what seemed to be another lifetime—Whitney had been in the mood for pasta.)

After a few minutes, I could hear the slow shuffling of footsteps. And the door at last was opened by a tired-looking older woman. With a belt cinched around her thin gray robe, she squinted out into the sun as if the dying daylight had caught her by surprise.

Then I looked again.

Wait a minute. That was Whitney.

"Oh, you look exhausted," I managed to get out when I had found my voice. "Please tell me there is something I can do to help."

Then Kate appeared to take the food, and she gave me a knowing look. "My mother doesn't sleep," she said. "I've been trying for so long to get her to lie down. But I'm so glad you're here. Please come in, come in!"

I moved into the den, with Whitney following wordlessly behind me, looking almost haunted. As I sat on the couch, I took in the scene. Two full garbage bags had been placed near the side door leading out to the garage. Several other bags of trash, half or two-thirds full, dotted the large room, and the space was also crammed with overflowing boxes and tote bags. In a lot of the boxes were little bits of paper, as if someone in the house had been going crazy with the shredder.

Whitney perched beside me at the edge of the couch, sitting as a person would when they did not have time to stay. "Rue." Her voice was a raspy whisper. "It was so nice of you to come, but I don't have much time, you see." She rubbed her fingers nervously.

Kate returned from the kitchen, where she'd left the lasagna, and sat down next to Whitney. "My mother thinks she needs to *shred*," she told me wearily.

"But…why?" My eyes moved from my friend to the boxes.

"All night she was up shredding, shredding." With her eyes, Kate signaled *Help.*

"Oh, yes, it's quite a job," said Whitney. "I've left it for too long."

Kate put her hand on her mother's arm. "Mom, it's time to rest. All of this can wait."

Whitney stood and moved toward a group of smallish boxes on a shelf across the room. She took out a pile of papers, rifling through them quickly. "Just a few more boxes," she mumbled softly to herself.

I exchanged a glance with Kate, then I went to Whitney and moved her back gently toward the couch, my arm around her shoulder. "Could Kate fix you some tea?" I asked. "Then we can talk a bit. Or would you like a nap?"

Seemingly too tired to argue, she sank onto the couch.

"Now." I touched her hand. "I hear someone has suggested setting up a scholarship—which Candace would have loved."

The mention of her daughter's name brought tears to Whitney's eyes.

"Why don't you get some rest," I said, "and then very

soon we can come up with ideas for a way to honor Candace."

In the quiet that came after that, I was overcome by how life had seemed to stop in that room, normally so full of chattering and excitement and ideas. And rather than the usual tasteful shades of blue and beige, it was all black and white, full of garbage bags and cardboard and messy piles of paper.

Then I heard a shuffling coming from the jumble of bags and papers beside my place on the couch.

I bent down to check it out, and between two stacks of paper, I saw a fat white tummy along with four black legs and a wet pink nose.

"Bud!" I stroked his tummy, which was his favorite thing for an admirer to do. I could have sworn he smiled, in that way a contented cat can sometimes seem to do. "Well, hello, sweet boy," I cooed. "Have you been here the whole time?" It was a measure of the chaos in the room that the most pleasantly rotund pet in town had managed to stay hidden in the midst of all the stuff.

When Kate returned with three mugs of tea, I asked her where the others were.

"Aunt Jean has run to town," she said. "With all of those Ackermans having been around for so long, we've run out of...you know, stuff. People have been nice—*so nice!* But instead of hams and casseroles, they could maybe bring, like…you know, dishwasher pods? And maybe toilet tissue?"

"That makes a lot of sense," I said with a nod. A sudden death might *seem* to make the world come to a stop, but life, in fact, went on. The power company still needed to be paid, telemarketers continued to light up your phone, and gas indicators still flashed their orange alerts.

Kate sighed and continued. "Uncle Matt has taken Laila to the beach for frisbee. Before he talked her into that, I don't think she'd left the house in days except for the funeral and the visitation."

"Matt has just been a godsend." Whitney stared into her tea. "In his looks and temperament, he's so much like the girls' father was. And here he is as always, doing all the things David would have done."

"Well, that *is* a lucky thing." I took a sip of tea.

"Oh, he's one of a kind, that Matt." Whitney had warmed up to her subject, but her eyes kept returning to the boxes, as if any moment she'd leap up and sort or throw things away. "They say going into business with a family member can tear relationships apart," she said. "But do you know the two of them, as far as I know, never had so much as a cross word between them? And Matt was always the 'big brother' to my husband even after they were grown. I never will forget how he once drove ninety minutes just to pick up David's favorite pie. It was for his birthday dinner."

"It was the same pie their mother used to buy him back in their hometown when they were growing up," said Kate. "Laila didn't want to leave her sketchbook for the beach, but Uncle Matt, he has his ways." A grin spread across her face.

As if on cue, the two of them came in, and Laila caught her sister's eye and smiled. "Yeah, he has a way," she said. "Like *grabbing hold of his niece's foot* and not letting go until I promised him that, okay, I'd go with him to the beach."

Matt Ackerman raised a playful eyebrow and pulled on Laila's ponytail. "The return of the foot monster. Who will not be disobeyed."

Laila rolled her eyes and filled me in on the joke. "The foot monster was a game my father used to play with me when I was *four years old*. And my uncle hasn't noticed I am all grown up." She gave him a playful shove.

"But did it work? It worked!" said Matt with a smile. Then he turned to us. "And let me tell you what, this girl can throw a frisbee."

"Thank you," Whitney mouthed.

Matt stuck out a hand to me. "Matt Ackerman," he said.

"Rue Collier. Nice to meet you," I told him with a smile.

"She has the Seabreeze Bookshop that we love in town," said Kate. "She can fix you up if you didn't bring enough of those books you like. You know, *Fifty Ways to Slay the Competition Before You Finish Breakfast.*" Then she turned to me. "That's the kind of book he takes *to the beach*. We need to introduce him to the concept of reading books for pleasure."

Bud was now at my feet, gazing up at me with rapt attention.

I must have misjudged Matt, I thought as I picked up the cat. The girls' now friendly uncle did look very much like the photos I had seen of David—although I never had the pleasure of meeting Whitney's husband. He had taken on the air of a legend in our town after the meteoric rise to success of Touchdowns and Home Runs, the chain of stores he and Matt had owned and run together. David had made sure no child in Somerset Harbor ever had to forego the pleasure of playing on a team because of a family's lack of funds. Uniforms and equipment were made available to all who fell below a certain income level. David often could be found throwing out the first pitch of the season in the local Little League.

Matt in the early days had moved to Maine to open

new stores there while David oversaw the management of the Massachusetts operations. Now Touchdowns and Home Runs were spread across the country with headquarters in New Hampshire.

We had visited awhile when I noticed Whitney had drifted to the boxes.

Matt followed my gaze. "I don't know what's up with that," he told me quietly, running a hand through his hair. "We're thinking maybe we should call her doctor. About some sleeping pills? To just get her to rest. In fact, I should do that now."

As he headed down the hall with his cell, Whitney rifled through some papers, throwing most of them into one of the million trash bags scattered around the room. It was almost like she was searching—desperately—for something.

Gently setting down the cat, I walked over and spoke quietly to Whitney. "Why is this so important? Is there something, Whitney, I can help you find?"

"Oh, no! Just cleaning up. Keeping tidy, they say, is the secret to a well-ordered home."

But the question seemed to scare her.

Something had been eating at her since the days before the reunion. Was there a key to murder buried in the piles of junk?

But if she understood that's where the answer lay,

she would have told the cops! No one would want the killer caught more than the victim's mother.

Maybe, I decided, the cleaning frenzy was an effort not to think about her loss—a grieving mother's way to pretend away the horror. Although denial by decluttering? That was odd and extreme.

"Whitney, let me help if there's something you must find." I put a hand on a box.

She looked at me with pleading eyes. "Rue, just leave me be, okay? I have to do this on my own."

She had to search—and, apparently, to destroy. My eyes moved to one of the boxes filled with shredded paper.

What was up with that?

I tried to catch Kate's eye, but she was staring out the window, tears streaming down her face. She was remembering, perhaps, some harsh words with her sister and wishing they'd had time to make things right.

Laila, in the meantime, had dived back into the comfort of her sketchbook.

So I quietly made my exit and left them to their ghosts.

CHAPTER SEVEN

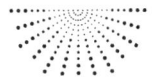

The next day I was shelving new arrivals when Andy called me back. I'd left a message for him, thinking he should know what was going on at Whitney's. As her friend I understood Whitney was a grieving mother, dealing with her loss in her own (decidedly non-Whitney) way. But to a cop, shredding documents could be a big red flag for "I have a lot to hide." And it just felt wrong not to let him know.

I went to my office for some privacy while I took the call.

"Thanks for telling me," said Andy when I had described my time at the house. "I think we absolutely need to get back in there and have a look. Or talk some more to Whitney. Because that behavior's odd."

Well, at the rate she was going, all they might find were shreds where stacks of papers used to be. Although earlier that day Kate had texted that the doctor had prescribed some pills to help her mother rest. So the shredder, I supposed, could cool down for a while.

"Right now, they've got me scrambling on another matter," Andy said, "but I will alert the chief."

"Making any progress?"

"Just some research on the knife, which seems to be a deluxe model of some sort. Not your normal weapon, so it's not that easy to track down who the maker was, how many of the things were sold, et cetera. There usually are markings, but this appears to be some collector type of thing with a silver leaf design. And an emerald on the handle! You don't see that every day."

"Interesting," I said. "Hey, Andy, do you know why Kate and her sister were at odds right before Candace died?"

"You know not to ask."

"I know, I know, I know. Confidential information," I said with a sigh. "Hey, look, I know you need to go. Find that killer, Andy. Candace was our girl."

"Full steam ahead on this one—with all hands on deck."

When I stepped out into the store, Elizabeth was

doing up a package in our special gift wrap, which featured pink and blue books against a yellow background. She tied a shell-shaped charm onto the package and gave it to the young man waiting at the counter. "I hope your wife will love it," she told him with a smile.

Gatsby, sitting at attention near the counter, let out a happy bark, adding his good wishes.

When the customer was gone, Elizabeth nodded toward her special corner of the store, where she sold old postcards, letters, photographs, and such, mostly from Somerset Harbor and the surrounding towns. "I've found a few things, Rue, you might want to see," she said.

As I followed her, I hoped it was something that could shed some light on Laila's scary drawing, which I'd told Elizabeth about. Although it was admittedly a long shot that Elizabeth could pull any hints from her inventory. The vibe was sweet and mostly happy at Antiquities by Elizabeth, a glimpse at the past through love letters, photographs of men in fedoras, and ads for penny candy. Crime and mayhem? Not so much, although she would sometimes buy collections of yellowing newspapers and old documents that had grown thin and fragile with the passing years. And sometimes those had tales to tell about the darker side of the town's past.

"I didn't go too far back," said Elizabeth, "since if the incident was real, it would have been, I guess, in Laila's lifetime—something she remembered." She picked something up when we reached her table. "But I did find this from six years ago." She held up a slick handout with the words "We Remember" written in black across the front.

Curious, I took the booklet from her and flipped through the pages. The family of a local drowning victim had, it seemed, set up a foundation to educate the public on staying safe in water. The last three pages of the full-color safety booklet were filled with the faces of local drowning victims along with their names and the dates on which they died.

"It's not a lot," said Elizabeth with a shrug, "but if we could find connections between any of these names and the Ackermans, I figured that might be a clue."

I looked especially at the faces of the men and boys, thinking of the drowning man Laila had felt moved to draw the day after Candace died. One photo in particular stopped my heart for a second. A thick strand of blond hair fell into the eyes of the young man, and it was his smile that nearly did me in. Dressed in a graduation cap and gown, the kid just seemed so joyful about the days ahead, days he wouldn't live to see. Around his neck, a mass of colored cords showed how much he'd aced his classes, how prepared he was to step out into the world and grab for what he wanted.

"Thanks, Elizabeth," I said. "This will be good to have." The cops, I guessed, would have a comprehensive list of drownings. And perhaps a way to see if any of them had involved the Ackermans as witnesses or friends. But I doubted that the sketch I'd seen and described to Andy would send them down that path.

"Oh, and I found these," said Elizabeth, spreading out some shots of Candace as a child and then a teen. There was no mistaking the expressive green eyes that had so expertly taken in everything around her. School hadn't held her interest. The world was way too full, she had always said, of more interesting things to learn. But despite her mediocre grades, she had been smart beyond her years.

"I bought a bunch of photos from a major sale about two weeks ago," explained Elizabeth. "It was put on by the heirs of a guy who apparently spent all his time behind a camera when he'd go to his kids' schools or to oyster roasts or the Merchants Guild Spring Fling, anywhere at all. I was thinking of a special theme for this month's display: Somerset Harbor in the Nineties. If somebody spots themselves, we could reward them with a bookmark or a small discount on a book—if you'd be up for it, of course."

"Of course." Elizabeth was full of fun ideas that always brought the traffic in.

I focused on a photo that seemed to have been made at a father-daughter dance. David Ackerman was dancing with a young Candace while little sister Kate was just a blur as she spun beside them in a circle. In another photo, the family waved from high up on a parade float. Candace and Kate were decked out in layers of red and blue sparkling beads. And David, according to a sign behind the family, was that year's grand marshal for the Fourth of July parade. No big surprise right there, given how much he donated to charities in town as well as to the schools and local efforts to beautify the downtown and the parks.

"I wish you could have known him," said Elizabeth, who had lived in town all her life except for four years away to get an art history degree at Smith. "He was always, well, just fun when you'd go in the store. Which makes sense I guess. Since when you think about it, that's what his stores are all about—giving people what they need to play the games they love."

"Whitney has always told me the girls adored their father." I studied the array of photos she'd found of the family.

Elizabeth let out a sigh. "So much loss in Whitney's life. I thought I'd fix a package of photographs for her.

The girls would enjoy them too—even though sweet Laila came along too late to enjoy the nineties."

It was Elizabeth's tradition to gift keepsakes from her stash to grieving families if she had any items that would be of comfort to them. She had stacks of boxes at her house as well as in the back room of the store, and she changed up her display with the seasons or simply on a whim.

"I'm sure they'd all love that," I said. Then something caught my eye. It was a photograph of Whitney and a toddler Candace in a tutu. It was a great shot of them both, but what got my attention was two figures in the background, almost lost within the crowd. The image of Matt and David in the corner was small and rather blurred, but I could make out that Matt's face was close to his brother's—and that his eyes were filled with rage.

I had seen that look on his face before.

"Did you know the other partner, Matt?" I asked Elizabeth.

"No, I never met him. He never was around much in the local store."

I scanned the other pictures and picked up the shot of the parade. And there Matt was again, in the back of the crowd. Standing at a distance from the other viewers, he leaned against a tree with his arms crossed, glaring at the float.

That man in the picture was so different from the one I'd seen the day before in Whitney's den.

And the look on his face chilled me to the core.

CHAPTER EIGHT

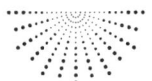

"We could have the girls write essays —*My Dream for the World*—about what they planned to do with their education." I looked from Kate to Whitney and then Laila as we sat on the couch. The opening discussions were overseen by Bud, who was next to Kate, lying on his back to invite tummy rubs.

"I like the essay thing," Kate said thoughtfully, leaning down to pet the cat. "Or it could be need-based. The counselors at the school could help us choose a girl who could set the world on fire but doesn't have the funds for college." She thought for a moment. "That would be a very Candace way to go, I think. Mom, do you remember how she used to give her field-trip money to the kids at school whose families couldn't send the fees for the museums or whatever?"

That earned a smile from Whitney. "Oh, but she made sure she got something for herself out of the deal." She turned to me to explain. "It took a while for me to catch on, but she would reward herself by skipping school on field-trip days. Figuring the teachers wouldn't miss her on the 'silent reading days' they always planned for those who were left behind."

"She would plan her own adventure." Kate shot me a small smile. "And there was even one time when the cops were called. Because she went to the shelter, snuck a pit bull out the back, and took him to the park."

Laila listened quietly and smiled while she sketched —hopefully a happy picture this time.

Two days after my last visit, Whitney seemed more rested, but her eyes at times still wandered to the boxes, which were still scattered haphazardly around the room. But someone had at least taken out the trash and neatened up the piles of junk.

"Mom, what do you think?" asked Kate. "Should it be need-based? Or should we do the essays? Or a combined approach?" Her gold pen was poised over her small notebook.

"Why don't you and Laila pick," said Whitney with a

smile. "Such a sweet idea, but my mind these days is scrambled."

I pulled my notes up on my laptop and continued, hoping still to draw her in. "Okay, I was thinking that instead of some plaque or piece of paper, we'd come up with something to give out more to the liking of young women. Like, I don't really think some wooden plaque is the kind of cool décor high school seniors dream about when they plan their dorm rooms out."

"I love that idea!" said Kate. She wrote it down in a pink cloth notebook, then she paused thoughtfully. "What would be a totally Candace kind of thing to sit on a dorm-room shelf?"

Laila shrugged. "A giant bag of Cheetos? A purple hair-dye kit?"

Jean breezed into the room with plates of red velvet cake. "Rue, I'll be packing up some of this marvelous dessert for you to take in for your staff. And we also have the most amazing marble pound cake. You should take some of that too so it won't go to waste." She sighed. "People are so kind, but you would not believe the food."

"Glad to help," I said.

"And tell Elizabeth we *so* enjoyed the photos." Jean set down some napkins. "Such happy memories." She touched her sister's shoulder before she moved back to the kitchen.

"What's new at the store?" asked Kate, sticking her fork into her cake.

"Well, I'm trying to get caught up with the modern world," I told her with a laugh. "I could do a whole lot more, I know, with my website, social media, and all of that good stuff. But it has been, well, a challenge."

"Oh, that's great," said Kate. "There's so much you can do now to build up traffic to your site and get attention for your brand. You could be selling books to readers from all over and not just here in Somerset."

I took a bite of cake, which was outstanding. "I am proud to tell you that I know…well, what SEO stands for. But beyond that, I'm kind of lost."

"You know that is Kate's thing, marketing and such," Whitney told me proudly. "And she was summa cum laude, so that should be good to pull in some more readers for your store."

"I'd love to help!" said Kate. She smiled at me shyly. "You've been so kind to us. In fact, if you want to work on it right now, I have really missed working with my mind since I finished school."

Once we'd finished with our cake, Kate took a bathroom break and Laila shyly waved good night before going to her room. When Whitney drifted to the kitchen, leaving me alone in the room, I snuck a look at the sketchbook Laila had left open. She had drawn a family—four women and a cat—inside the outline of a house. But the house and the family had been broken into pieces and scattered about the page, like so many pieces of a puzzle.

And then Kate was back, insisting that we both take our laptops to the kitchen table, where I pulled up my current website and the one I had started building. Kate got right to work, helping me figure out which "keywords" my target audience was most likely to type into Google. Then I watched, amazed, as my friend's young daughter became a machine. Her mouth was set in a firm line as her fingers flew across the keys, adding the "magic-ticket" words and phrases to my dummy site. A move that would hopefully bring my website higher on the list of search results.

"Just some ideas," she said, "to show you how it works. You can play around some more with the copy to get it the way you want."

For her next bit of wizardry, she suggested I create a presence in the corners of the web where book buyers liked to hang. We pulled up a few of my favorites, and she suggested I add comments when I could on their message boards. "Write your stuff in such a way that they know you're an expert when it comes to books," she said. "And don't forget to link your comment to your site."

As we continued with our work, Matt came through the kitchen, nodding a hello and cutting a piece of cake for himself. I was aware of Whitney in the next room, moving back and forth between the boxes. At times she looked almost desperate as she frantically pulled out paper after paper, creating massive piles. Every now and then she'd disappear into a back room, where the sound of the shredder formed a background to my work with Kate.

"Kate." I looked at her, concerned, when the shredder started up again. *"What is going on?* What is in those boxes that your mother wants?"

"Oh, believe me, I have asked!" Kate looked to be near tears. "I don't know what to do! How to help my mother." She twisted one of her long curls around a finger. "Oh, Ms. Collier, it's so weird. Now all the stuff we need—like our current mail—is mixed up in those boxes she's pulled out of the closets. So, what if there's some bill in there that isn't getting paid?" She looked down at the table. "And she's been in my room and Laila's, grabbing our stuff too."

"Oh, Kate, I am so sorry." It was much worse than I thought.

"It's, like, in this house, there's no privacy at all. Some of my stuff is…well, just gone. Which in this kind of mess means impossible to find. Maybe I should have majored in one of those kinds of fields where they do excavations and dig up buried stuff."

Jean appeared at that point, as if she had been summoned by the misery of her niece. "I have your mother's pills," she said quietly to Kate. "Let's you and I tag-team it and get her off to bed."

Kate gave her a nod, and soon they each had Whitney by an arm, shuffling her off to her room. Whitney by that point seemed tired enough to go along.

I stood up from my chair and stretched, taking a few minutes to rub Bud on the tummy. He cocked his head to watch me. "You know, I'm pretty sure nothing gets past you," I whispered to the cat. "If only you could talk!"

Trying to appear oh, so casual, I walked past the piles and boxes, taking little peeks at the pages on the top. Having just watched Kate taking notes, I was pretty sure I recognized her loopy cursive on a sheet of paper.

Six Important Things to Know

If for any reason you hear that I'm gone, take my pink skirt as a gift from your BFF. And please rescue my plants, because no one at my house will give them any love.

You're too smart to ladle soup into bowls all day for tips. Med school, med school, med school.

Before I could read the rest, Kate came into the room.

"She's asleep," she said, looking relieved—and very normal. Not like someone who was collecting high-tech gizmos to help her vanish from the world.

"Hey, I have an idea," I said. "Why don't I take some of these boxes and go through them at home. You know, to make sure nothing vital has gotten mixed into the jumble. Like the power bill. And maybe your mother would calm down if there were fewer boxes to pull at her attention. This…task that she feels compelled to do might not seem so overwhelming."

"You would really do that?" Kate asked me, wide-eyed. "That would be amazing."

I was a little shocked the crazy plan had worked.

"I think it would be best for me to grab those over there, closest to the kitchen, near where you keep the bills." That would mean I'd also get the note from Kate and hopefully more stuff from her room that had been grabbed at the same time. It felt uncomfortable to invade her privacy, but the secrets in the house could unmask a killer; how could I not look?

We headed to my car with our arms full, and soon we had filled the back and trunk with reading material for the evening and beyond. I had a feeling it would be a late night fueled with lots of coffee and very little sleep.

CHAPTER NINE

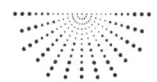

My plan had involved my comfiest pajamas and that pot of coffee as I searched the tote bags and boxes for an answer. Something in the haul might reveal why Kate had been fighting with her sister. Or what had fueled the rage I'd glimpsed in Matt. Somewhere in the boxes spread across my floor might be an explanation for Whitney's odd behavior.

With so many vital questions swirling in my head, I found I couldn't wait, even for caffeine. Instead, I dug right in, first reaching for the letter, the possible "goodbye" to Kate's friend.

And there were more of them: the starts of cursive heartfelt missives to about a dozen of her pals. In the letters Kate gave voice to the kinds of things that friends might think but keep to themselves so as not to micromanage, not to overstep.

Buy the airline ticket. Tell the boyfriend to get up and wash the dish himself. Grow your hair out, wear more red. And in case she never said it, always know how much you are loved by Kate, who adores your laugh, your ability to listen (kind of a lost art), or the way you weren't afraid to ask a stranger if he might be that guy from *The Voice*.

I closed my eyes and breathed, grasping at any explanation for why Kate might have a wish to up and disappear. She would surely understand what it would do to Whitney for another daughter to be gone from her life.

Well, perhaps the answer could be found in a box, so I dug in again, pausing for a moment to chuckle at the cats, who seemed thrilled with the new "toys" I'd brought. They were batting happily at the wrinkled coupons and floral sticky notes that had fallen from a bag with their reminders and an excess of exclamation points. *Schedule manicure and Botox!! Check the roast at six!!*

Next, I shuffled through a bunch of normal household stuff that should have been organized or thrown out years before. An old receipt for tickets to a play at the Glove and Garter here in town, printed-out instructions from the web on how to get a wine stain out of silk, a lot of to-do lists. *Buy orchids and ornamental cabbage. Bottled water, chicken breasts. Refresh sun porch cushions.*

I picked up a list of names followed by phone numbers, and I recognized a couple. Bess Katz was in the Wednesday book club at the Seabreeze, and Jake Smitherton came into the store a lot to stock up on the detective series that he liked to follow. Both of them were lawyers specializing in white-collar crimes. The kind of jobs you joked about: *I hope I never need you, so I guess I should behave.* I could tell the list had been written not that long ago. Because one of the names had a date followed by a question mark.

Two weeks before Candace died, someone in the home had been scrambling to get help from a lawyer about some type of fraud or shady business dealings. Whitney was still somewhat involved in decisions about Touchdowns and Home Runs. Had she crossed some kind of line?

I had hoped for answers. Instead, I got more questions.

The next box was filled with mostly useless junk. Why had Whitney held on to a receipt for three mugs and a candle from six years before? A reminder that Bud was due for shots in 2015 or an application for a craft show that had been over for six years?

I stifled a yawn and stood up to stretch, deciding that the time had come to make that pot of coffee. Or since it was well past midnight, it was really time for bed. But I was not the type to go to sleep with all kinds of possibilities just waiting at the bottom of a box or stuck between old notes.

Beasley mewled for help, and I bent to pull a sticky note off of his paw. Ollie had apparently tired out and commandeered an empty box to take a nap, and he soon was joined by Beasley.

While I got the coffee going, I went out to the car for four more boxes.

And it was in one of those I managed to rescue the stack of recent mail, which would be a relief for Kate; I'd text her the next day. I looked through what appeared to be old notes from the recreation board, then I found a catalog from Touchdowns and Home Runs from 1989, and something on the cover caught my eye. It was a knife with a hand-forged leaf design on the silver handle and a green jewel near the bottom. Exactly as Andy had described when he talked about the knife used to murder Candace.

The description touted that this was a "T and H limited edition," T and H being the name of the store's premium collections. "Very Limited Supply," warned a note beneath the picture. Which was probably a good thing since a limited number of buyers would pay the listed price.

Given this rare weapon that had been made and sold by the family business, there seemed to be very little chance Candace had been murdered by a stranger. I looked again at the picture of the knife, which appeared to be more of a work of art than a weapon—although there *was* that sharp blade.

"An heirloom," said the advertisement, "to be passed down to the next generation."

Or to murder them.

CHAPTER TEN

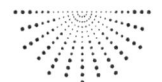

*L*uckily, a lot of customers came in the next day to distract me from the fact that I was functioning on about three hours' worth of sleep. There was a threat of heavy rains all week, and since so many in Somerset Harbor spent a lot of time outdoors, customers needed books to tide them over till the sun came out again.

Knowing we were in for a busy day, Elizabeth, Beth, and I got to work right away setting up a display in the front: "Our Staff's Favorite Books for a Rainy Week." We mixed paper clouds and yellow rain boots among the chosen books. And in the spirit of inclusion, the pets got picks as well. They were, after all, an important part of the bookshop family. I smiled to myself as I set Gatsby's photo in front of the book he was "recommending," *All Creatures Great and Small.*

I was straightening up a cloud when Baxter Ridley entered, throwing his hand up in greeting. "Okay, ladies, hit me up with your best science fiction," he said with a grin. "Although it's the truth that will scare you more than fiction if you look too closely, right?" He raised a playful brow.

I smiled. "I think I can find some stuff that has your name all over it."

He followed me to a section in the back of the store. "I meant to call you back," he said, "but then I saw the forecast and thought I'd come on in and get some books." He leaned against a shelf and watched me. "So, have you finally decided you might join us for a meeting? Count yourself among the prudent, the most likely to survive?"

"If I did decide to come, what would it be like?" I asked. "Just me and a bunch of guys?" Or, in other words, would a recent college graduate named Kate be likely to show up for some tips on how to vanish?

"Well, it's mostly guys." He laughed. "But we behave, I promise. And if you graced us with your presence, we'd refrain from burping loudly and engaging in offensive male behavior." He crossed his arms over his chest. "But, seriously, Rue, you are not the only female who has shown a recent interest in what we have to offer. You should come on out. We could set you up with everything you need to survive—and thrive—in your choice of hideaway."

"Any other women that I know?"

Baxter cleared his throat. "Well, the thing about it is, we have a prepper's code. So I really shouldn't say. Now, some of us are open about the things we do. There are those of us who feel it's important that we spread the word—to get ready while you can." He jammed his hands into the pockets of his khaki shorts. "But there are others, Rue, who come to us for advice, and they would just as soon we keep that interaction to ourselves."

"So there are *secret* preppers?"

"Well, think about it, Rue." He leaned in close to me, warming to the subject. "Let's say disaster hits, and almost no one in the population has enough to feed their families. People would be desperate, right? And then the word gets out that you have in your basement a hundred cans of soup! Some people might do anything to get at your supply. So for a lot of people who have worked hard to prepare, that secrecy is vital."

"Hideaway!" the shop parrot screamed. "A hundred cans of soup!"

"Okay, well, I see." I took a breath and began to pull some books for Baxter to consider.

But he was just getting warmed up. "And, Rue, you have to understand that a day could come when access to a doctor will no longer be a given. When you can no longer count on the availability of things like contact lens solution, for example, or an extra pair of glasses." He rested his pointer finger next to one of his blue eyes. "Which is why last year I got LASIK on these babies."

"Oh! I had no idea, it was so…involved," I said.

Then I saw that quite a line had formed at the counter, where Beth was ringing orders while Elizabeth was helping a young couple in the memoirs and history section.

I handed the books I had picked to Baxter. "Well, it looks like I should open another register," I told him. "Why don't you browse through these and let me know if you need more. Everyone has raved about the one on top."

It was after noon before I felt I could take a break to update Andy. I slipped into my office, punched in Andy's number, and, thank goodness, he picked up.

"Hey, Rue! Not much time. The chief has me going in eight directions all at once."

"I can just imagine. But I have a few things I thought might be of interest."

"We'll have to make it quick. I have an appointment

coming up, and I'm still tracking information on that fancy knife. Or trying to, at least."

"Well, you are in luck. Because about that knife—"

"And I need to press the chief on getting in to see those boxes. Because time is of the essence if she's shredding left and right."

"You see, that's another thing! Because I've had a chance to—"

"Based on what you've told me, there could be some *crucial* evidence in there—that could make or break the case. And it might be getting shredded even as we speak." His voice rose in frustration.

"But the good news is that yesterday—"

"But does the chief of police take the time to listen? No!"

"Yesterday, Kate gave me permission to—"

"Those boxes, Rue are—"

"In my house! They are in my house!"

"Wait. What did you say?"

"Andy, I have the boxes. Well, not all of them—but about fifteen."

That was followed by a pause. "But how?"

"Kate was so frustrated by the way her mom would not sit still—when Whitney needed rest. So I made the offer to whisk some of them away. And Kate told me okay."

"Well, why did you not say?"

"I tried!"

"And here I was just rambling on about the boxes. And the mystery knife."

"Which was manufactured by the company owned by the Ackermans. That was the other piece of information I was trying to get out!"

There was another pause. "Okay, Rue, I'm all ears."

With Beasley winding around my ankle, I updated Andy on the knife and about the fact that someone in the house had been searching for a specialist in white-collar crime shortly before the killing.

"And Kate has been writing notes that sound to me like goodbyes."

"That's a whole lot to take in," said Andy with a sigh. Then after a pause, he added, "That was some fine work, Rue."

I thanked him and hung up, feeling very sleepy.

The night before I'd gotten through all of the stuff from Whitney's except for one large box and a big canvas bag. Anxious as I was, I'd brought the bag to work in case I got a moment to go through it. And that moment might have come, judging from the heavy rain now pounding on the window. The promised storms had started.

A quick peek out my office door confirmed that the

downpour had resulted in an empty store. So I grabbed the bag and shuffled through some old receipts and photos, a few grocery lists, assorted household papers, and a bunch of scribbled notes. *Kensington Blue, Three Gallons. Pick up alterations.* I wondered how many to-dos in that house had turned into not-dones, lost in all the stacks.

Then another picture slipped out of an envelope. The handsome teenage boy with longish hair looked familiar to me. A customer perhaps?

Then a loud clap of thunder sounded, and a Beasley-Gatsby-Ollie blur raced underneath my desk amid mewls and whines.

"It's okay!" I told them, putting on a playlist with Adele and Kenny G, the kind of smooth, emotive music that seemed to soothe my furry trio best.

Then suddenly it hit me. The kid in the picture—he was the drowning victim I had seen in Elizabeth's handout. Had he been the one on Laila's mind the day after Candace died, when she had lost herself in that piece of art?

It would have been an odd response to her sister's death, given that the drowning had been six years before —when Laila was a child.

But I had a name, at least. Another trail to follow.

CHAPTER ELEVEN

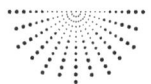

The next day promised to be our only break that week from the rain. So I took advantage of the clear skies to run to the bank and then to First Impressions Stationery, where I had ordered bookmarks with the address of the new website. Hopefully, having them all ready to hand out would inspire me to keep working—and I could launch my new site soon.

Still on the south side of town, I was on my way back to the bookshop when a familiar figure strode into my view, walking down the sidewalk at a quick, determined pace. As I got a little closer and stopped for a light, I could see for sure that it was Matt. Curious, I followed his progress as he made his way to the gates of the Hobson B. Anderson Nature Preserve and Trails.

With its quiet walking paths and scenic salt-marsh

views, it was the perfect place for a grieving man to spend some time alone. But judging from the way he kept looking at his watch, my guess was that his plans involved something very different than meditation and reflection—which meant it was a perfect day for a curious bookseller and her dog to take a little nature walk.

Gatsby had ridden along with me for the two quick errands, and he'd be more than thrilled to spend some time at one of his happy places. But this time we wouldn't focus on the horseshoe crabs and native birds that made this a beloved haven; this time, it was a human male I planned to track down and study.

"Change of plans!" I said, pulling into the parking lot. "I think both of us could use a little exercise."

Gatsby's joyful howl showed that he agreed.

I parked and grabbed the leash, noticing that a lot of families had come out to enjoy the reprieve from the rain. A small crowd to blend in with could work in my favor. The impromptu plan was to observe Matt from a distance without him observing me.

We'd walked about ten minutes, Gatsby trotting happily ahead, when I spotted Matt. Half hidden behind a thick patch of trees, he was firing off a stream of words at a thin young woman as he glared into her eyes. She appeared to be somewhere in her twenties, with a thick mass of long red hair streaked with lilac. She stood very still, defiant, her arms across her chest. But when the sun broke through the treetops, I could see the gleam of tears just beneath her eyes.

I put my hand on Gatsby's neck, which was my signal to him to keep quiet. He was on alert, his eyes intent on the confrontation, and I knew his instinct would be to protect the girl.

I moved behind a birch tree, getting as close as I dared, and I tried to listen. I could only catch a few words, however, and mostly they were Matt's: *Have to have it now . . . Do it for your friend . . . Necessary for the family.* His tone made the remarks seem more like an order than like a request.

Then before I knew it, he had moved back onto the path and was stomping toward the exit. I quickly turned my back in case he'd remember meeting me. I was in no mood for hello, and from the looks of it, this bully of an uncle was feeling the same way.

"Come on, boy, let's go," I said quietly to Gatsby, who was focused on a group of diving, splashing loons. Reluctantly, he turned his back on the show and came.

We walked around a bit before returning to the spot where Matt's "victim" had remained. Fingering a gold chain around her neck, she was sitting on an iron bench staring blankly at the water. Very quietly, I took the place on the other end of the longish bench.

So much I'd loved to ask! But, of course, I doubted she'd be up for a chat. This was a woman, after all, who had just been stared down and intimidated by an entitled jerk. She probably needed space—but Whitney and her family needed answers.

I pulled a paperback out of my bag and settled back against the seat, staring at its pages, although, to be honest, who could concentrate? Gatsby settled at my feet, and I reached down to rub behind his ear. My best hope for information was probably my furry walking buddy, who could turn a stranger into a BFF with one thump of his tail. As if on cue, he gazed up at her with a sympathetic whine, his head resting on his paws.

A smile tugged at her lips. "I used to have a dog who looked a lot like that. I can tell that he's a sweetie."

"This is Gatsby," I said as he made his way to her for a head rub. "He loves to come out to the trails any chance he can and pull me away from work."

"Well, Gatsby has good taste." She gazed at the water, which held a reflection of white light as it filtered through the trees. "What a gorgeous place," she said, petting Gatsby. "But they need to have a sign: *Scumbags Not Allowed.*"

I tucked my hair behind my ear and frowned. "Did someone bother you?"

She let out a sigh. "It's my own fault, really, for even coming here when the guy asked if we could talk. But how was I to know the uncle of my best friend was a major creepazoid?" She kicked at a rock. "My friend who passed away." She paused to shake her head. "And Candace always told me this guy was so great! He really had her fooled."

"Do you need some help?" I asked her gently. "What did this guy do?"

She waved away the offer. "He's just one of *those* guys, you know? Who's used to giving orders and people just obey? I had never met him until not that long ago. But, well, you can tell he is that type—who always has to be in charge."

"And the guy was giving *orders*—to *a friend of his niece who died?*"

"Well, not so much an order as a strong 'suggestion.' But this is not a man who is used to hearing no."

"Whatever did he want?"

She fingered her necklace nervously. "I don't want to say a lot about that ugly conversation. Because even now, I have taken in too much of his bad energy, you know?" She closed her eyes and breathed. "What I want to do is release his vibes from my inner being and take back my peace." She paused for a moment. "But he's basically insistent that he get his hands on this little trinket that used to be my friend's. I have it in my purse; I was gonna say okay. But once his attitude came through, no way was I gonna give that cretin something really special that my friend had loved." She gave me a small grin. "So I said I didn't have it. And I believe the powers of the universe would smile on that little lie."

She rubbed Gatsby's head as he sniffed the overfull brown purse lying on her lap. "Do you smell peanut butter?" she asked him with a smile. "I believe I have some treats, because I always meet some dog friends when I come here to walk." After looking to me for permission, she reached into the bulging bag, pulling out a candy bar, lipstick, some tissues, and a phone until she found the treats. She held three out in her hand, and Gatsby eagerly scarfed them down. Then he rubbed his head against her knee, his way of saying thanks.

"It's just the weirdest thing," she said thoughtfully. "Because my friend *adored* her uncle. And now my friend is gone." She cocked her head at me, a question in her eyes. "You probably read it in the news—Candace Ackerman?"

"Oh, I know all about it. Her mother is a friend. A heartbreaking situation. I used to always love it when

Candace came into my store. I thought the world of Candace."

"Candace was the best."

We were silent for a moment, lost in our thoughts.

"If he was her uncle, you'd think he would be grieving and not following her friend around to basically harass her," I said with a raised brow.

My new friend shook her head. "Oh, this guy sees himself as some kind of hero who can somehow make things better by tracking down this little trinket. Which is really super weird." She creased her brow in thought. "Honestly, I think the man has lost his mind."

What had I overheard him tell her? *Necessary for the family.*

"How did he think that would help, this trinket?"

"He really didn't say. And I didn't ask. All I really wanted was for him to shut up and leave."

"And what kind of object was it?"

She just shook her head. "To speak more of the man might invite bad spirits into my safe space, where I come to calm myself. I must speak healing words instead. *Compassion. Understanding. Double-chocolate brownies,*" she whispered to herself.

We sat quietly for a moment as Gatsby lay his head on my foot and dozed.

Then she stood to go. "It was nice to talk with you," she said, "to see a friendly face after all of that."

"Well, I'm sorry for your loss. I'm at the Seabreeze Bookshop if you ever want to talk."

Once she had been gone for a few minutes, I stood up as well and tugged on Gatsby's leash. "I still have a store to run," I told him, "so I guess we should get back there and…maybe sell some books?"

He stood up sleepily, but instead of walking with me, he sniffed at the nearby bushes. Apparently, some of the treats had fallen out when his new friend pulled the treat bag from her purse.

"Aren't you the lucky one?" I said with a laugh. He gobbled up two treats and then batted his paw frantically beneath a bush for more.

"That's enough," I told him. "Too many treats can hurt your tummy."

But Gatsby was persistent, and soon he was easing a small statue from the brush.

"What do you have there?" I asked, bending down to pick it up. About the size of my palm, it was an intricately carved likeness of a lion. The creature was all white except for a silver mane.

This exquisite little guy must have fallen out of the woman's purse when she was pulling out one thing after another to get to the bag of treats.

Was this what Matt had wanted? What an odd thing to seek out.

Oh! And the woman from the park would be devastated when she found out it was gone, since it seemed to be a link to her lost best friend.

I took it with us to the car, where I wrapped it up in tissue, placing it carefully into an old box that once held business cards. Maybe Kate or Whitney could help me find the friend and I could return the treasure.

I glanced back at Gatsby when I pulled to a stop at a light. "Weren't you the ace detective?" I said to my good boy. "You might have found the clue that will break the case right open."

Although I could not imagine what the clue might mean. Did the white lion know the secret behind the horror in the pool house? His head was lifted back in a mighty roar, but if he had any answers, he was keeping that information to himself.

CHAPTER TWELVE

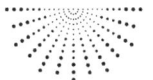

Back in my office at the shop, I turned my focus to the website. I clicked on the section at the top that was titled "About Us," and I told potential viewers the story of my gran. One day at the beach she had finished reading Toni Morrison's *The Bluest Eye,* and she found herself without another book to grab. She had decided then and there it was a crime for there not to be a bookshop located nearby. Our lovely stretches of white sand and gorgeous water were too much of a bookworm's paradise for the town to go without.

I wrote about the beloved summers I'd spent as her helper at the store while Judy Blume and Charlotte Brontë did their part to help me navigate my childhood and the tricky teenage years.

"Make it personal," Kate had emphasized. "The Seabreeze isn't any bookshop; it's a place with heart, so make sure that comes across."

I had found a photograph of Gran and me setting up a display for a summer reading program. Lyle, Lyle the Crocodile was smiling from the cover of one of the selections, and Amelia Bedelia too. It took me back to that sense of freedom and anticipation of early summers on the beach when June, July, and August still stretched lazily ahead.

As excited as I was about the project, though, I couldn't concentrate. My mind was stuck on my final memory of Candace in the store, her face lit up with laughter as Gatsby ran to greet her. I could not stop puzzling over the jumble of odd facts that refused to tell a story that made any kind of sense: the search for a criminal attorney before Candace died, Kate's apparent need to get away, the drowning boy, the angry uncle, the much-sought-after regal lion. Which clues were important? Or were they all just odds and ends of a family's life, unrelated to the murder? Everybody's family history could be messy if you looked close enough.

I placed the photograph of me and Gran into the dummy site and remembered something she had told me long ago. My friends had planned a last-minute bonfire when I was fourteen, and a certain boy was almost sure to be there—a Justin-Bieber lookalike who had returned my shy smiles in a way that made me think that might be the summer of my first great romance. And yet...I had picked up *The Yearling* for the first time that year, and as the story took some devastating turns, I couldn't bring myself to put the book away until I knew the end.

The bonfire or the book? And if I picked the book, did that qualify me as a helpless nerd?

Gran—who could read my mind in a way that was sometimes scary—had some advice for me. "Sometimes when a story calls to you," she said, "you have to push through to the end. And when you finish the last chapter, the beach will still be out there. And so will the boy."

And now I was feeling the same way. I had to find the end of the tragic story that had broken all our hearts. And this time, unlike with my beloved fiction, I could maybe make a difference in how the story ended.

I let out a deep breath, feeling that I had Gran's blessing to take a little break from updating the website. It was important to me to take good care of her store while she traveled and tried out new hobbies during her retirement years.

But where in the world to start in puzzling out the

murder? There were so many loose ends that might lead to the killer—either that or send me flying off in the wrong direction. As I closed out the website, an image of the drowned boy popped into my head as if to say "Pick me."

As good a place to start as any.

"Okay," I whispered to him, and in my head, he looked on solemnly, as he had in the picture I'd pulled out of the junk the Ackermans had saved.

I brought up Google on the screen. "Jason Lavelle, who were you?" I asked as I typed in his name.

What I found was a lot. Apparently, the drowning had drawn a lot of coverage from the local press, and I pulled up several stories. The well-liked football star, it seemed, had been accepted into Harvard, where he planned to study physics. There had been a lot of questions at the time about how the avid swimmer could have drowned in Starling Lake on a sunny, breezeless day. He seemed to have been alone at the small lake at the time.

Next, I googled Matt and found several photos of him accepting honors on behalf of Touchdowns and Home Runs. Apparently, the business had become a leader in supporting youth-related charities and mentoring their young employees. Matt in interviews gave his late brother credit for the focus on giving back to the communities that had supported them, beginning with the year they bought the local store where they had been employees. Quickly after that, they had expanded to multiple locations.

With no more answers (or even any hints) about the questions surrounding the tragic loss of Candace, I pulled out my notes from Kate to think some more about my website. As she had advised, I checked out other bookstore sites, choosing stores I knew enjoyed vibrant online sales. One of my assignments from my young advisor was to come up with ideas that would set me apart.

But all that seemed to do was leave me feeling overwhelmed with how high the bar was set. The sites were splashed with gorgeous, professional-looking photos of artful merchandise displays. There were interviews with local authors and even a recipe for chili from a "Cookbook of the Week."

I closed my eyes, feeling daunted by the challenge of the website, the lack of answers in the case, and, most of all, the heartbreak that had descended on the town. I could hear a buzz out in the store and knew it was filling up; I needed to get out there and work the floor with Beth. But first, I decided, I'd shoot a text to Kate, who was on my list of worries. It was hard enough to lose a sister, but what an extra blow for her—to have just exchanged harsh words with Candace. She had seemed reluctant to talk about their rift, and I knew it wasn't good to hold things like that inside.

And something else was off with Kate, I thought as I picked up the phone, something that went beyond her family's tragic loss. Maybe she and I could take a walk after work before the wet weather hit again.

"Sure!" she texted back. "Can you meet me at six at the college science building? Next to the front door? And don't even ask—or you'll spoil the surprise." That was followed by a winking emoji.

Intrigued, I sent back a thumbs-up. The small but well-respected Campbell College was not too far from the store, and I had worked some with the staff there on book-related programs.

Time flew after that as I rang up orders and helped customers find books. The cash registers stayed busy as did the table with hot tea, which Gran had put in to invite customers to linger.

Then before I knew it, it was close to six, and I set off for the college, where I parked my car and hurried down a tree-lined path to Aster Science Hall and Observatory.

Kate was sitting on a stone wall next to the complex. She jumped down and grinned. "It's a nice, clear night. Care to see some stars?" she teased.

My heart skipped a beat. "Can we really get in? Because that would be amazing." Except for select occasions, the pricey equipment in the observatory was reserved for students only.

"We are cordially invited to view the skies above." Still grinning, Kate dangled a key from her fingers.

Now that I thought about it, Kate Ackerman *of course* would have access to the building. Donations from her father were probably the reason the college could afford to even have the observatory.

So we made our way in and spent an exciting evening looking at the stars. Kate, to my surprise, turned out to know the sky about as well as she knew her way around the web.

"My father used to teach me," she explained when I complimented her vast knowledge. "We'd come after dinner. Sometimes Candace would come too, but a lot of times, it would just be me and him. It became our thing."

Through the pricey telescope I saw Jupiter up close with its bands of color. I saw what appeared to be a mass of blue-white diamonds, which Kate explained to me was a star cluster called Pleiades.

"Just magical," I said, feeling awed by the hugeness of the world above me. And by how much of its beauty went unseen by us.

As the night wore on, I was glad to see the place seemed to bring a sense of calm to Kate. She was different here: quiet, and more thoughtful. Her dad had left his middle daughter the gift of a place in which she could find her peace.

She pointed out some constellations we could see with the naked eye. As a little girl, she had chosen the queen Cassiopeia as "her" constellation. She showed me how the stars seemed to form the picture of a seated lady.

"Because come on, really. Who wouldn't want to be her?" she asked me dreamily. "A lady in a chair, watching from the sky."

"And this whole time," I said, "I had no idea she was there." But now that I'd been shown her outline, there she was—so clear.

"And some nights when you look up, she'll be sitting upside down, which I always thought made her extra cool," said Kate. "Hey, you need to pick a constellation too. My father, he loved Leo, and he could recite all the stars in the constellation: Regulus, Algieba, Zosma..." She smiled softly at a memory, and her voice grew quiet. "He would name each one in this kind of loving voice—like he and they were friends."

We lapsed into silence as we watched the sky, and I could feel the stirrings of something shifting in me, a new openness to life. First, I would let Kate transform me into the kind of person who could master the wide world of tech. Then I'd become the kind of person who had a favorite constellation, and I would look up to my "sky friend" when I needed strength.

"Then after my dad died," continued Kate, "I still had Leo up there, looking out for me." She let out a sigh. "His lion in the sky."

Yes! Leo was *the lion*. I had been too entranced by the stars to make the connection. The statue Candace loved must have been her father's—or a gift from him. The silver mane had almost glittered, as if the mane were made of stars.

"In my mind sometimes, the lion came alive," said Kate. "A big, friendly sort of guy. And then, of course, one day I looked him up, and I saw the story. That he was some fierce creature who had a bunch of women trapped before Hercules came in and killed him. It was my first lesson, I suppose, that things aren't as they appear."

Now that I thought about it, the lady in the sky was no benevolent, watchful presence either if you were familiar with her story. She was, in fact, banished to the sky for being such a braggart about how beautiful she was.

But did it matter, really, what the myths had to say?

"The beauty of a story," I announced to Kate, "is that we can always make it into anything we want." And so in my mind, it would always be a good-hearted lion and a kind lady in a chair who looked down on me. Earth could be a challenge, and I needed friendly skies.

My mind went back to the statue. "Did Candace feel the same way?" I asked Kate. "About the lion in the sky?"

"Probably she did. My dad was always saying we should go out and be lions or grab the lion's share. 'Inside every woman is a lion,' he said all the time, and I ate it up. But that kind of rah-rah-rah really wasn't Candace. She just wanted to enjoy, you know?" She was quiet for a moment. "But our father came to understand, I think, that my sister was fierce in her own way. She just had other causes besides building up new streams of income, bottom lines, and all of that." She closed her eyes, and I saw a sparkle of a tear. "And I get that now, but before I didn't. There were a lot of things I misunderstood about my sister."

"You know, Kate, people like your sister get that they are loved, even in the times when they are maybe not so close with someone they care about. Because of all the years that came before and all of the good times."

The utter stillness of my friend let me know she had disappeared inside her head; I was not about to get a clue about the reason the two had been estranged. But maybe she would say some more about her Uncle Matt.

"Like your dad and uncle," I said to her gently. "I know they were super close. But being in business together like they were, I'm sure there were disagreements."

"You would think, but no. There was only one time I really heard them fight—not long before Dad died." A darkness moved across her eyes as she remembered. "Uncle Matt that day had come over to the house, which was kind of a surprise. He wasn't living close, and we had no idea he was coming." She stared straight ahead. "I was across the street that day with my mom and sisters. The neighbors had a new pool they wanted us to see. But I started feeling bad, and I decided not to swim and just to come on home." She looked me in the eye, and I could see the pain she felt. "It was an awful day, Ms. Collier. My uncle kind of went ballistic, which really freaked me out. Because he was not that way."

"What was the fight about?" I asked her gently.

"Well, I didn't hear a lot; I could hear his tone more than I could hear words. Because once I saw his expression, I ran up to my room and shut the door. I had to get as far away from him as I could."

"Did your dad talk about it later?"

"No, he never did. But for the longest time after that

awful day, he'd get really quiet. It got to him; I could tell. All I could overhear was something about golf clubs…and maybe about bikes? It seemed like normal stuff about the operation of the store, things that were no big deal." She paused for a moment. "A lot of things about that day were weird," she said thoughtfully. "Like, he wasn't in his Porsche. He had come to our house in this smallish van—the kind you use to move stuff? So maybe he was on his way to somewhere else." She shrugged.

"Did you ever ask your mom about it?"

"Honestly? I just wanted to forget and pretend it didn't happen." She looked down at her clasped hands. "But now I really wonder what was going on." She thought for a moment. "You know, I *did* hear Uncle Matt say the name of a lake on the other side of town. Which was also weird. Because even if they weren't in the middle of some fight, the two of them would never, ever take time off of work to go to Starling Lake. They sold fishing poles but never took the time to use them."

My breath caught in my throat. "Did you say Starling…Lake?"

There he was again, the boy. It all had to be connected. Because Starling Lake was small, as opposed to one of the more popular recreation spots Matt might choose to name at random. And if the argument had happened not long before David died, the time frame would fit.

My mind began to spin with unrelated facts. A statue with a starry mane; the "accidental drowning" of a strong, athletic swimmer; tension between sisters—and between brothers too. Wondering what it meant, I gazed up into the sky. Which—despite all our science and all our explorations—kept so many of its mysteries to itself.

CHAPTER THIRTEEN

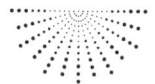

The next Monday was my day off. So I spent much of the day huddled with Kate at the Ackerman kitchen table, crossing off our checklist for the website launch. I admired the way she attacked the project with a fervor. It was a distraction for her, I supposed, and that was good.

She wouldn't let me pay her. But between website tasks, I was pitching in to get the house into some kind of order in the wake of Whitney's purge, which still mystified us all. But Kate had reported that her mom was losing steam—and was sleeping well most nights with the help of meds.

Every chance I got I would skim the tops of the remaining boxes for…well, for any kind of hint of what was going on.

"Still no clue what she's after?" I whispered to Kate in the late afternoon as I swept some bits of paper from around an empty box.

"No!" Kate was breaking down a box, and she glanced at me, worried. "But she worked most of yesterday in Candace's old room, which is still jam-packed with stuff. And I could tell some of the things in there just sent her off the edge." Kate's face had turned pale. "It honestly was scary how upset my mother was. And I think she's in there now."

"She is having such a time," I said with a sigh.

"A whole lot of that stuff had been cleared already to make room for Uncle Matt, but that was just a dent," she said. "A ton of it was left."

The problematic uncle had left two days before to get back to business, so Whitney had begun to concentrate on that room in her cleaning frenzy.

I paused with the broom. "It might be hard for her to be there with your sister's things right now," I said quietly to Kate. "You don't know how much I wish she would just be *still* and take some time to grieve."

"Well, at least it's getting better." Kate pulled her hair back into a knot. "Who knows what my mother is unearthing in that room. There's some stuff from the stores in there, I think. Because when he worked from home, my dad would use it as an office." She gave me a wry grin. "And there's assorted junk from my mother's crafting projects. Because no one in this house seems to have learned the art of *throwing things away.*"

At a little after five I ran out to the Methodist church to pick up barbecue from the Kiwanis Club, who were raising money for their Children's Fund.

Whitney, her eyes red and puffy, seemed especially distracted as she nibbled on her pork.

"Kate has been such a help with my new website." I was trying hard to keep the mood somewhat cheery. "Plus, she introduced me to some constellations. Which I, of course, had heard of. But no one ever showed me how to find them in the sky."

"If you had ever been outside with my dad for *two seconds even* on a night when the sky was clear, you could point to the lion." Laila dipped her fork into her beans. "Oh, man, did he ever love his lion made of stars."

"And there was a quote about a lion for any problem you might have." Kate exchanged a playful glance with Laila.

"Like, there was this one time I was scared to take piano lessons," Laila told me. "I wanted so much to learn, but I hated the idea of those recitals, which they always made you do. And I was way too shy. But my dad, he said to me if you don't do some things that scare you, you will just cheat yourself out of your best life.

And now piano playing kind of takes me to another place, piano and my art."

"And I bet he used the same old lion quote that he did with me," said Kate with a laugh. *"Have the courage of the lion; the whole jungle can be yours."*

Whitney suddenly pushed her plate away. An angry look was forming on her face, taking the rest of us by surprise. "That lovely sentiment is all well and good," she said. "Except from the viewpoints of the toucans and the rhinos and the monkeys. What does it mean for *them* when the lion wins the day, taking what he wants?"

After a momentary silence, I was the first to find my voice. "I'm sure he meant it in the best way, in the sense of going out to chase your dreams and all of that. Not in the sense of harm."

Laila looked down at her lap. "He was the good kind of lion—who helped a lot of people."

I took a bite of slaw and changed the subject to the scholarship. "We'll need publicity," I said, volunteering to call the local media once we'd hammered out the details.

"And I can talk to my counselor at school," said Laila, "and she can promote it to the kids." But there was no enthusiasm in her voice; the mood was spoiled.

When no one had taken a bite for a while, I stood up to clear the table, and the girls jumped up to help. As we cleaned the kitchen, I told them how I'd met a friend of their sister at the park. "She dropped something I found later and took back to the store," I said as I dried a dish. "I was thinking if you knew her, you could let her know. I didn't get her name, but maybe she's the only friend with red and lilac hair?"

"Oh, that's our neighbor Steph," said Kate. "Steph is really cool. I will let her know for sure."

Then the three of us moved into the den, and Laila grabbed some trash to take to the curb. "Thank goodness the trash people come tomorrow." She gave us a wry smile as she headed to the door.

"I think we'll all feel better when this room gets back to normal—or somewhat normal anyway," Kate said with a sigh. She shoved the remaining boxes into a corner of the room. *"And what's up with my mom?"* she asked in a low voice. "Aunt Jean is freaking out. Today she went to see some friends near Chatham, but when she gets back, she is going to *force* my mom to get out of this house."

I swept the cleared space clean, having to move carefully around the big cat Bud, who seemed to be entranced with the movements of the broom.

Kate looked at him and laughed. "Bud really isn't used to this weird thing called 'cleaning,' which is not a thing that happens that much in this house. All of this is new to him! Of course, we have the maid. But he likes to hang out with Mom in her room when the maid is here."

With his head tilted to the side and an intense look in his eye, Bud watched the sweeping action as I worked. Often he would plant himself in the very spot I was planning to sweep up. Then with a sudden movement, he would reach out to catch the broom in mid-sweep.

I bent to rub his head and smiled. "Did you find a new toy? Maybe Kate and Laila will bring it out again, and the three of you can have a game."

When I finished sweeping, I saw Laila frowning down at several boxes filled with shredded papers.

"If you'll grab more garbage bags," I said, "I'll throw those shreds away, and we can flatten out those boxes." But what I really wanted was to get inside that old home office that had become a room for Candace. Whitney had headed back there as soon as we'd finished dinner, and I could hear the whir of the shredder.

What had Whitney found that had been so upsetting? Had Candace left behind a clue? Or had Whitney discovered something in her husband's business papers that distressed her? From all accounts, the two of them had been married happily, so her outburst at the table had seemed to come out of nowhere.

I thought back to the days before the fateful family

gathering around the pool. Well before her company arrived, Whitney had begun to spend time in her husband's former office—to clean it up for Matt. And in those pre-reunion days, she had seemed distracted when she came into the store. Had she even then started to find things that upset her?

That would have been about the time someone in the house made a list of lawyers. The very type of lawyers who might advise a widow with connections to a business in which lines had been crossed.

But how could that have led to the murder of the oldest daughter? Any clue I found seemed to circle to that question, and I had no answers.

Laila came back with some trash bags, and she and I got busy bagging up the shreds. Kate had an inspiration for the website and ran to her laptop while I bagged up trash.

We were hard at work when Jean breezed into the room on a wave of perfume, her arms full of shopping bags. "Rue! So good to see you, dear," she said. Then she turned to her nieces. "Let me put this stuff away, then I will grab your mother. I've texted her already to get dressed, that we are going out." With an apologetic smile, she added, "Oh, and I told her, Kate, that you were coming too."

"Well, okay, sure. I guess," Kate said with a shrug.

Jean looked her in the eye. "I told her that as much as she was hurting, her girls were hurting too. And that you really wanted to see *Little Women* at the movies. And to see it *with your mom.*"

"And I do!" said Kate. "Because she and I read the book together—twice." Then she turned to me. "Why don't you come too?"

"You go take a break and let me finish cleaning up," I said. "You have helped so much with my website, and it's the least that I can do." The den was looking better, but the dining room was filled with empty boxes to be flattened and trash to be taken out.

Plus, there was a room to search.

"Okay. If you're sure," said Kate gratefully. "Laila, come with us."

"That movie's not my thing," said the youngest daughter. "I can help Ms. Collier and maybe draw a little too."

"That would be fine," said Jean, knowing Laila needed space and the comfort of her art.

About fifteen minutes later, I heard the three women leave. Whitney, I could tell, was reluctant, but I might have also heard the softest giggle. I knew Whitney's giggle well, but that sound had been absent from my life for a while. The magic of some good girl time with family might have begun to crack her deep sense of despair.

Once I heard the car start and pull down the drive, I headed to the former office space of one David Ackerman. I couldn't wait much longer to get into "the" room.

CHAPTER FOURTEEN

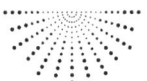

"I'm going in the back to do some cleaning," I told Laila, who'd retreated to the safety of her pencils and her sketch pad.

She gave me a nod, and I thanked the universe for the magic ticket into what I hoped would be the room with answers.

What I saw at first was a lot of Candace—framed photos of her on the beach with friends, a collection of alien figurines I vaguely recognized from some show I'd read about. Boxes had been pulled out of the closet and were in various stages of being emptied out, while papers and file folders were spread across the bed.

Mostly what I found were assorted papers associated with the business: payroll records, canceled checks, bank statements, all of that. I plopped down on the bed and thumbed through the first stack, scanning some of what I found. But there was nothing there that would have panicked Whitney; this was all normal stuff. I picked up a second stack and looked through some outdated proofs for ads and some drafts for contracts that appeared to be pretty standard.

Then I threw them to the side, disappointed at the lack of a hint about what was going on. For the love of Banquo's ghost! Something interesting had to jump out at me before the credits rolled on Jo March and her adventures. After that these papers, I was almost sure, would have a date with a shredder.

Then I came across a folder with a handwritten note across the front in large red letters. "TO BE KEPT IN HOME FILES ONLY," it almost seemed to shout.

Now, that was worth a look: something David Ackerman hadn't wanted other eyes to see. The first paper I pulled out seemed to be a receipt for products: golf clubs, sneakers, bikes, and fishing poles that had been delivered to the store here in Somerset Harbor. Nothing suspicious about that, although some of those prices on the sneakers—whoa. The only other paper was a receipt as well. It was dated the same day in 1988 and listed the exact same items—but in bigger numbers. I pulled out my phone and grabbed some photos of both the receipts.

I sorted through some more normal-looking stuff until a name on an invoice caught my eye: Harold Ackerman. That was the oldest brother, an insurance adjuster in Vermont. Whitney used to tell me how her husband had enjoyed teasing "Hal" about how rich he could have been if he had joined the company when Matt and David went from employees to store owners in 1992. But Harold had famously stuck to his guns about not mixing family with business.

On a hunch, I grabbed some papers I had set aside and pulled out some payment records. And there was his name again. Numerous payments had gone out to Hal throughout the late eighties with notions such as "consult" or "equipment."

Time for more photos on the cell.

I stood up and stretched and went to the kitchen for some water, mulling over what I'd found. Back when there was one store only—here in Somerset—Matt and David Ackerman had worked their way up from sales clerks to management before they bought the store. Then expansion had come right away with one grand opening quickly following another. Business journals had covered with great reverence the brothers' meteoric rise.

I leaned against the counter and took a long sip of water, then went out for some air, wandering to the back where I could have a clear view of the stars. I had to rest my mind, and maybe Kate's big sky could bring me peace as well.

Then something caught my eye; it was a suitcase-shaped bulge in a shed beside the pool, and I headed over to investigate. Yes, it was a suitcase, packed so full it looked to be about to burst. What was it doing in the shed with pool-cleaning tools and floats, a stack of paperbacks, and towels? Beside it was a soft overnight bag, also bulging, in a blue Vera Bradley pattern, and there was a tote bag as well, stuffed full of books and papers.

I took a deep breath. These could not belong to Jean, who was due to stay another week (and who would have no reason to keep valuables out in the open, unsecured). Kate had said she'd be there when I hit "publish" on my website, that we'd go on out for drinks. But when that day arrived, would Kate have up and disappeared?

A sense of dread swept through me. I had no idea where all the clues were leading, but I feared the heartbreak in that house might not be over yet. With my own heart pounding, I found the lion in the sky, willing him to bring me courage. "Inside every woman is a lion," I whispered to myself. Then I headed back into the house.

In the den, Laila was still sketching, and I could tell that she'd been crying. I moved away to give her space, but she looked up at me and nodded toward an armchair. "Sit down and take a break," she said. "You've been going at it hard."

I took my place across from her and gave her a gentle smile. "Well, we're making progress, and I'm glad."

Tears began to stream down her face. "This is just the worst!" she said. "We need her to be here."

I moved to the couch beside her, and Bud jumped up to lay a paw on her leg.

"I am so sorry, Laila," I said in a quiet voice. I could not imagine the hole left in her life by the loss of Candace.

"I know you must feel so empty," I said softly. "That you must have a million things you want to say to her."

"Oh, yeah, I do! I really do. Like I want to tell her that right now is the worst time to run off to Alaska. Because we need her here."

Oh! She must mean Kate. Which made a kind of sense. Kate would have given her little sister a heads-up rather than surprise her with a second loss.

And Kate was going to Alaska?

"She thinks I don't know," said Laila tearfully. "But she left her computer open when she left for the show." She looked over at me with a desperate look. "And she had pulled up flight times. Flight times for next week!

Airfare for *one person!* And not even *round-trip* airfare, so who knows when she'll come back?"

So—it would be the next week. I felt stung but kept calm. "People grieve in their own ways," I said. "This might be the thing your sister needs to heal, to have some time away."

"Oh, I don't mean my sister. I meant my *mother's laptop*." Laila threw aside her sketchbook. "And did she even plan to tell us, or did she just plan to go?"

CHAPTER FIFTEEN

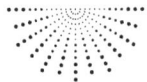aila wiped away a tear. "I'm so mad at my mom. *Because I need my mother now.*" Looking much younger than her sixteen years, she gave me a pleading look. "Aunt Jean thinks she's on the verge of some kind of breakdown. Because first she loses Candace, and then she starts in with this weird cleaning frenzy." Laila gently stroked Bud's fur, then the tears came even harder. "She can't go off alone! She can't. Because she isn't well."

I touched Laila's arm. "I'm here. Kate is here and Aunt Jean. We'll make sure your mom's okay," I said.

I closed my eyes, still stunned—and confused. Despite the zillion projects that always kept her busy, Whitney Ackerman's first focus had always been her girls. No way would she leave them now—unless there was something pulling at her she truly felt was urgent.

There was clearly evidence in David's office that the origin story of the business was more sordid than the version paraded in the press. The two young employees who had bought the first store and "dreamed their way to success" had stolen and cheated their employers first. Whitney in recent days might have found some evidence of fraud that shocked her. Or maybe, as wives often do, she'd long ago seen beyond the PR version of the man she'd lived with for so long.

But that was not enough to explain her odd behavior. Or the need to run.

Whatever the story might be, my concern for the present moment was this youngest daughter, who had crumbled into a ball at the end of the couch. We found a movie for distraction and Laila, somewhat calmed, picked her sketch pad up again and drew until we heard the moviegoers returning in the foyer.

Whitney went straight to bed, but Jean hurried over when she saw her niece's face. "Honey, what is wrong?" she cried.

In a rush of words, Laila told her aunt and sister what she'd come across on her mother's laptop.

Kate went white, sinking down onto the couch, while

Jean put a hand over her mouth, a dark look in her eyes. "Oh!" Jean's voice was hushed. "She surely didn't mean it." She reached for Laila's hand. "We all have our ways to escape—in our minds, of course—just as a mental break. But I assure you that your mother would never leave you girls." She looked from one girl to the other. "Not even for a few days, not at a time like this when all of us are reeling."

I stared down at the carpet. Jean was right up to a point; we all dreamed of escape. But unless we had plans to truly disappear, we didn't pack our bags and stow them out of sight.

"Let me make some tea," I said, rising from my place. Not that filling a warm mug could ease this kind of sting, but one brings out little comforts when they are all one has to give.

Kate nodded, blinking away tears, and Laila reached again for her sketch pad. The strong and mournful movements of her pencil seemed to be a conversation with the page open on her lap.

When I passed through a little later with the tea, I could see a face taking shape on Laila's page. Getting closer to the drawing, I was startled by the intense stare of a boy. And then I looked again. Oh, my—it was *the* boy. Once so joyful on the day of his graduation photo, Jason Lavelle now watched me solemnly, his eyes seemingly reflecting the sense of horror we all were feeling then.

"Such a handsome boy," I told Laila quietly as I set down the tray of tea.

Kate looked up, curious, and wandered over for a look. "Laila," she asked her sister, "what made you think of Jason?"

"Because I'm tired of losing people." A tear rolled down Laila's cheek, and soon both girls were crying.

"He was perfect, right?" Kate said quietly. Then she touched her sister's shoulder. "I think I'll turn in early." She spoke in an almost whisper and made her way to her room.

Jean picked up a mug and took a sip. "He and Kate were high school sweethearts," she explained to me. "Both of them were smitten. It was a *youthful* love, of course, but I think that one would have lasted."

Laila gave me a sad smile. "Kate would not have dared to break up with Jason—because I would have beat her up."

"For this one here, our Jason was just like a big brother." Jean nodded toward her niece. "He loved to bring her little treats when he came to pick up Kate."

"And he'd tell the best stories," said Laila quietly.

"And the intelligence of this young man was just extraordinary," added Jean.

Laila looked up from her drawing. "If Dad could have picked out anyone for Kate to date, he would have dreamed up Jason. He was into business like my father and was always asking questions about increasing profits, diversifying products, all of that. While me and Kate and Candace? We didn't really care about that kind of thing, even though my father wanted one of us to grow up to be the CEO of Touchdowns and Home Runs."

"I always had the feeling David had his eyes on Jason as a future leader on his team of execs," said Jean. "He was supposedly a sales clerk, but David was always pulling him back into the office to research products, talk strategy and sales, and even to write up the history of the company for a new brochure. He was grooming him, I'm sure, to help lead the business once he had his degree. They were a lot alike, those two. They could have built themselves some empires as a dynamic duo, except..." She let out a sigh.

I raised my brow in a question.

Jean hesitated for a moment, staring at the carpet. "Except that Jason drowned," she said.

Laila stared blankly at the page. "I think I'll go to bed."

She rose, and I nodded my good night while Jean kissed her on the cheek. Bud scrambled from the couch, where he'd been sitting next to Laila, and nestled up against my calf.

"That is just horrendous." I took a sip of tea. "Those poor girls—so much loss."

"And the timing of the thing made it even worse," Jean told me quietly. "Just before Jason died, there was a massive fight. Right here at the house—between him and David." She paused with her mug halfway to her mouth. "I happened to be here at the time, and I had never heard such a nasty tone coming out of David. It was really bad."

I sat up a little straighter. "What was the fight about?" I asked.

Jean just shook her head. "We never really knew, but I never will forget. They were standing by that closet at the end of the hall, which I believe that Jason had mistaken as the restroom, since those rooms sit side by side." She paused, lost in thought. "I did hear Jason say something about some kind of theft. Which never made a lot of sense—since there had been no losses that we knew of." She narrowed her eyes at the memory. "And then David seemed to almost *shout* at the poor boy that something or another was none of Jason's business." Jean let out a sigh, staring down at her clasped hands. "Very unlike David, who was always encouraging the young people on his staff to be curious, to ask questions, and to learn."

"What did Jason say?" I asked.

"Just that he saw some work stuff and thought it was okay to look—since David had him working on a history of the stores. He said some other things as well, but that was all I could make out," she said.

"How did Kate react?"

"Thankfully she wasn't here. She and Jason had just come back from the beach, and she and her sisters had run out to grab a pizza."

Could Jason have discovered the same information that had caused Whitney to wig out? I thought of the paired receipts for items that had—supposedly—been delivered to the store back when Matt and David were employees. With the same dates and the same items, the only difference I had noticed was the *numbers* of golf clubs, bikes, sneakers, and other pricey stuff. Had the brothers been using the extra items for their own gain, in effect stealing from their bosses? They had to have been up to something fishy, or David would not have marked the folders to be kept in the home files only—underscoring the importance of the warning with his choice of a vivid shade of red felt-tip pen.

Bikes and golf clubs, I remembered, had also been

mentioned in the fight that Kate had overheard between her father and her uncle not long before David died.

Still, I couldn't help but think I must be missing something. With the despair I'd seen in Whitney, the fury with which David had gone after Jason, I sensed the crimes must run deeper than those early thefts.

I thought back again to the fight Kate had overheard between Matt and David. Matt had been incensed and showed up without warning. Something huge was clearly up.

And they had mentioned Starling Lake, I remembered with a chill.

A scenario began forming in my head.

And it was horrific.

"Did you say they were standing by that closet when the fight began?" I tried to keep an even tone when I spoke to Jean.

She picked up her mug. "Oh, yes. By the restroom in the hall. Like all the other closets in this place, it's crammed full of ancient stuff that no one's bothered to clear out in years—or maybe decades."

"Be right back!" I said. "Before I head back home, I need to run to the restroom."

But first, I might "by mistake" open the door to the closet that sat next to the bathroom. And if I got really lucky, I might spot what Jason saw not long before he died.

Fortunately, Jean was facing away from the bathroom I did not intend to visit right away.

"Go right ahead," she said, gathering the tea tray. "I'll be in the kitchen cleaning up. And then I need to shoot some emails to my husband and my daughter. With this situation with my sister, I'll have to extend my stay."

Aha. With Jean keeping busy, I'd have more time to explore.

CHAPTER SIXTEEN

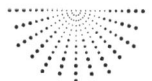

The smell of dust let me know right away that Whitney hadn't made it to the closet by the restroom in the course of her purge. A thick coat of dust rested on a box near my feet, and big flecks of the white stuff wafted in the air. Three fishing poles and a bag of golf clubs were shoved against the back, and I could see a sales tag dangling from one of the fishing poles. A couple of full backpacks had been leaned against the wall, and a shoebox was half open to reveal a pair of black and white Nike shoes.

Bud, who had scampered behind me as I walked down the hall, pawed at a discarded flashlight in the middle of the closet.

In one corner was a small filing cabinet, and I had to

have a look. Quietly, I shut the door. Even with Jean being occupied, I didn't have much time.

Bud let out a meow as he rolled the flashlight with his paw, and I nonsensically held a finger to my lips—as if the cat would conspire to keep my secret by playing quietly. When he continued with his noisy game, I carefully opened the door, moved the flashlight to the hall, and Bud ran out to play. Then I shut the door again.

One of the folders had been left on the floor, its scant contents spilling out. Picking up the papers, I found bills for a storage unit located in Wellfleet, about a twenty-minute drive from town. Along with the bills was a handwritten list of names. Beside each name was a date, a time, and the name of a piece of sports equipment along with a price.

"Are you okay in there?" Jean called from the kitchen.

Shoot. I had to hurry.

Careful not to make a sound, I opened the door, moved to the bathroom, and called out from there. "Thanks for checking. Yes, I'm fine. Just a little tummy trouble." Then I snuck back to the closet, where I might allow myself maybe two more minutes. Bud looked up from his place in the hall, where he was still happily rolling the flashlight in a circle.

Back inside the closet, I moved to the cabinet and

pulled out a folder with a stack of lists similar to the first one. *Rick Jordan, May 2, 2:15, MacGregor clubs, $350.*

I reached for a second folder and found pages of classified ads torn out of local papers. A yellow highlighter had been used to mark ads for sports equipment. "Brand new. Never used!" touted the advertisements. The address of the storage unit was listed as the meeting place for the exchange of goods for cash. The phone number at the bottom was for a local number, but the ads had been placed in papers for surrounding towns, never Somerset. David and Matt had been careful to keep their dirty business away from local eyes—well, except, I guessed, for Jason's. Maybe the folder on the floor had been what he was looking at when the fight began with David.

Bud, who had apparently grown lonely, began mewling at the door, and soon a black and white arm appeared through the door crack, sweeping the floor for treasure.

Now, I really did have to get out of there before Bud alerted Jean. But I had seen enough. It was not the crime I'd meant to solve, but I had a good idea of why a local boy had "drowned" mysteriously on a sunny day in a calm and tranquil Starling Lake.

The next day I summoned Andy for some early-morning coffee on the porch and filled him in on what I'd learned.

He let out a low whistle. "That does sound like some solid evidence against the brothers in the drowning death. And the widow's packing up to leave?" He rubbed his chin to think. "This is one crazy case. That is useful information. Thank you for that, Rue."

Of course, he wasn't willing to give me any updates on the case in exchange for my news. So later at the store, I was left to speculate about what might be going on as I tried (and failed) to do some work on the website. First up on my to-do list was to find a bookish quote to go across the top of the home page. I needed to arrange for someone to take my photo, and I had been assigned to come up with what Kate liked to call "fun facts" about my life.

"But it's about the store, not me!" I had said in protest. I'd already put a photo of me as a child with Gran on the "About Us" page. Did viewers also need a photo of the grown-up me?

"People have a choice about where to spend their money," my personal website guru had explained. "And rather than throwing money at some random, impersonal-looking site, don't you think they'd prefer to give it to a friendly-looking woman who loves yoga on the beach?"

"Except I don't do yoga," I said with a laugh.

"It's only an example," Kate told me with a grin. "And I do yoga every morning—sometimes on the beach. You should give it a try."

I tried to think of a "fun fact," but my mind kept wandering to the case. Andy had given me no hints that the cops were about to solve the thing, and I felt driven to help find the answer—for Whitney, for Kate, and for Laila.

I had found some clues about a mystery from the past, but that did not point to a reason for a killer to go after Candace six years later. The clues did not explain those packed bags of Whitney's or her sudden need to flee. Her late husband, it appeared, might have been more crook than hero. But those were his crimes, not hers.

Jason's death and Candace's—had they even been connected?

There were so many pieces of the puzzle that still didn't fit. Like why had Andy mentioned a collection of supplies for preppers? Was Whitney, with her packed bags, planning to live off the grid, in some remote place out of touch? Once upon a time her idea of roughing it had been to skip her manicure.

And why had Matt insisted on getting his grubby hands on that statue of the lion?

I thought of my favorite literary sleuths: Sherlock Holmes, Hercule Poirot, and other geniuses from our shelves of mysteries. For them, the key to solving crimes was not only in asking the right questions but in finding the right source for the answers. I had spent a lot of time with several of the Ackermans, but what about Jason's family and friends? They might be able to clear up a lot of things if I could get to them.

A quick Google search brought up the old stories from the time of his death. I found some quotes from his mother, whose name was Lorraine Lavelle. Then I typed her name into the search bar and found out that she owned a photography studio, Captured Moments by Lorraine, on the east side of town.

How perfect could that be? Kate thought I should have a professional photo taken for the website, and who better to take that photo than Lorraine? Perhaps I could make some headway on this investigation and move forward with my website all at once.

I called her right away and explained I was building a new website. "My advisor thinks I need a photo that makes me appear to be likable and unique," I said with a rueful laugh.

"Oh, that's part of what we do," said Lorraine, whose

deep, rich voice seemed to hold a smile. "With our business customers, it's our job to show our subjects in their best light: competent and approachable."

After I described the store and my business, she proposed that we meet on the beach, where she could take some pictures of me and Gatsby too. Kate also had suggested that the pets be a big part of the site. They were, after all, important members of the bookshop family. And including Gatsby in my photo should shoot my "likeability" way up. Who wouldn't want to buy a book from the world's most handsome and big-hearted, happy dog?

"Hey, you might be in luck," said Lorraine. "One of my customers has come down with strep throat, so a time slot has just opened up for tomorrow at five thirty. The lighting should be perfect at the beach at that time of day if you happen to be free."

Beth was scheduled to be at the store to close the next day, so I could make that work.

"Let's do it," I told her, and we made a plan.

First, Lorraine took some posed shots with me and Gatsby by the water. Then she gave me a big smile. "Now that we've got some good ones with your hair looking nice, we can try some candids with the wind-blown look," she said. Then she photographed us playing. I'd throw a stick for Gatsby, and then the two of us spent some time chasing the surf.

"Beautiful!" Lorraine called from behind the lens. She was a big woman with the same blonde hair and kind eyes as her son. But even as she laughed at Gatsby's antics, I could see a hint of darkness in her eyes, and I knew that came from a loss that would always tug at a mother's heart.

Once the photos were done, the sun had begun to set.

"I love this time of day," I said. The golden ball up in the sky had dropped to the point that it almost seemed to touch the water. "Gatsby always loves a walk at sunset," I said. "Would you care to join us?"

With her hands on her hips, she gazed up toward the sky. "You know, I think I will. I could use the exercise. Just let me lock up my equipment in the van."

"Sounds good, and I will grab my leash."

We kicked off our shoes and strolled along that magic point where the tide sometimes took you by surprise, rushing across your feet with its salty coolness. I told her how I fell in love with the area visiting my gran as a child. She told me in turn how her family had moved here from Vermont when her husband was transferred by the consulting company he was working for.

"We divorced soon after that, but I decided I would keep the charming beach town even if I didn't want to keep the man," she said with a smile. "And then I needed money, so I thought I'd do what I love—which is taking pictures. It's something lasting I can do. Because moments, they don't last. The people that we love the most…well, you never know when they'll be taken from you. But all the photographs of the happy times? At least those are forever."

The sun by then had disappeared, and the water had a pink glow that tonight seemed melancholy.

"I think we feel it most at sunset, the losses we've been through," I said.

"The saddest time of day, I have always said. And yet this is the time of day you kind of feel them near. I lost a son, you know. He had just graduated, had his bags half-packed for school; he was on his way, and I have to tell you, that kid had the biggest heart—and he was a genius. Although he didn't get his smarts from me or his father. It's a mystery, you know: how two ordinary people could produce a modern Einstein. And how he loved the beach! Ever since he was a kid. And it's here I sense him most."

"Oh, I am so very sorry. That must be a loss that you feel every day."

"Someone killed my boy. Some would tell you that he drowned, but the cops confided in me they think someone took his life. They just don't have any proof."

"Lorraine, I have no words. Do they have any clue about who did it? Or a motive? Anything?"

"No, they really don't. But, you see, here's the thing. Jason always carried with him this little statue of a lion. Which I know sounds like an odd thing for a teenage boy to do. But it was given to him by a mentor who meant the world to Jason—a kind of good-luck charm. I was always after him to leave the thing at home. You would not believe how much money Jason's boss spent on that little gift, and what if it got lost?" She bent to pick up a shell. "But I know he had it with him when he went to Starling Lake the day he died. There was something on his mind that day, and he told me 'Mama, if I walk out by the lake, I can clear my head.' The lion wasn't in his backpack, which they found on the shore. Someone who knew its worth must have taken it with them along with Jason's wallet, which was also missing." She let out a sigh. "I know that it's a long shot, but the cops have always told me if they ever find the person who has Jason's lion, there would be a strong chance that person killed my boy."

My chest seized up at her words. *Candace* had the lion, which she had given to a friend just before she died.

Stunned, I could barely breathe for several awful moments.

What could it all mean?

"How many people knew?" I asked. "I mean, about the lion."

"That was always something the cops kept close to the vest. So just the family, I think. Oh, and Jason's girlfriend; I believe they told her too. They were just the cutest couple."

And the girlfriend's older sister, I imagined, could have known as well. Because sisters like to talk.

And something just before her murder had told Candace to whisk the lion out of sight.

CHAPTER SEVENTEEN

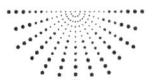

The next morning, I was at the counter working on an order for new books when the bell on the door signaled a new customer's arrival. I had passed the morning in a state of dazed confusion, mulling over the latest puzzle piece.

And then, as if by magic, the Ackermans' neighbor Steph was striding toward me. Here was the very person who might have some answers about how Candace came to have the pricey lion.

"Thank you a million times for finding that little statue that I dropped," she said in a breathless rush, a wide smile on her face. Then she bent down to pet Gatsby, who seemed drawn to her stacks of dangly bracelets. "I could not believe it when I got back to the house and saw that it was gone," she said. "Candace gave it to me to hold on to the last time that we talked." A sadness crossed her eyes. "So that makes it really special. Like a piece of her, you know?"

I pulled it out from beneath the desk, where it waited, nestled in a box and wrapped in tissue. "It's a lovely little statue." I chose my words carefully. "Do you know where she got it?"

"No idea," she said with a shrug. "But it seemed important to her. She just came over one day and asked me to keep it safe."

"Keep it safe?" I asked.

"I didn't ask her what she meant," said Steph, "because that day was super weird. She seemed in a rush to get back home, and I could tell that she'd been crying. There was a whole lot going on at the Ackermans' that week. Her uncle had just gotten into town, and they were all getting ready for the reunion thing."

I nodded toward Gatsby, who had settled happily at his new friend's feet. "You can thank your buddy for the rescue, because he's the one who dug your prize out of the bushes."

She bent toward the dog. "Did you rescue my lion? Are you my handsome hero?"

"How very odd," I mused. "What could that have meant—to *keep it safe*?" Of course, if it was evidence of murder, she'd want to keep it hidden. But why the sudden urgency after all these years?

"Maybe she wanted me to keep it safe from the creepy uncle?" Steph rubbed Gatsby's neck. "At the nature trails, the man certainly was eager to get his hands on the thing. Probably because it's worth an insane amount of money. Like, would you believe a statue that *fits in the palm of my hand* would cost more than some cars? I remembered the name of the manufacturer on the foot of the lion, and I looked it up when I got home from the trails that day and found it gone. So maybe Candace worried that it might get broken with all the company gathered in the house." She shrugged.

"Did she seem upset that week?" I asked. "Before she came over with the statue?"

"I didn't see a lot of her right before she died. She was kind of on a mission, cleaning up her space so the uncle could stay there. Candace is no neatnik, but most of the stuff in there is from her dad's old office, which is what the room used to be. A few years ago, her mother turned Candace's old room into a space to do crafts. So when she moved back this time, she took the old office, which always had the best views and the most space, all of that."

While Steph moved on to browse the new releases in fantasy and science fiction, I mulled over what I'd heard.

Had Candace found the statue among her dad's old business stuff, and had she understood what it might mean? And did that knowledge get her killed? Although David was not around to answer for his actions, Matt seemed to have a lot to hide as well. Which could have been the reason that he sought out Steph when he figured out she was holding on to evidence he would want destroyed.

How far would he have gone to protect the reputation of his business?

Beasley jumped onto the counter, and I rubbed his back, imagining what might have run through the mind of a scared young woman entertaining tough suspicions about a beloved parent. Perhaps her mom had confided in her about the explosive confrontation between Jason and her father not long before Jason died under suspicious circumstances. And upon discovering the lion, Candace might have suspected the unthinkable regarding Jason's death. Perhaps she took her fears to her trusted uncle—but it wasn't comfort that she found with her longtime father figure.

It was just a theory, but the pieces fit.

I was lost in thought as a text came in from Kate. Apparently, Aunt Jean was taking both the sisters to the Lobster Fest the next day; it was an annual tradition on our downtown streets. Since they didn't want to leave Whitney by herself, they were dragging her along.

"Uncle Matt is coming too," she wrote. "He is coming back today to help us figure out the weirdness with my mom. And I guess we all could use an outing. Hope to see you there!"

I was already planning to be there in the morning. The bookstore had a booth featuring some favorite seafood cookbooks. Both Elizabeth and I would prepare some sample dishes, and we would hold a drawing for a basket filled with books, scented candles, and flavored tea.

But now I would stick around when my morning shift was done. I had a few questions for Kate's Uncle Matt, and it was best I ask them surrounded by a crowd for my own protection.

CHAPTER EIGHTEEN

*A*s I arranged my books and food on the display table, the festival staff had begun to gather along with an early crowd. A salty breeze promised perfect weather, but the day felt far from a celebration. I waved at Reg from the men's store and watched as some unlucky volunteer dressed as a giant lobster mingled with attendees.

As I set out some crackers by the crab dip, I noticed that the bright red lobster had a familiar slow and bouncy stride as he headed over for a sample.

"*Andy?*" I asked, my mouth hanging open. "Aren't you…well, a little *busy* for an acting gig?" I had texted him the night before that I had another update, but I had not heard back.

Now, he held out his claws in a sign of helplessness.

"After all the late nights at the office, the chief just decided I needed some fresh air to clear my mind. But this case is exploding. And I need to be at work, even though my mind is fried."

"*Fried* can be a good thing in a lobster," I told him, holding back a smile.

Andy rolled his eyes, his face showing through a small peephole in the costume. "Plus, we have a booth: *Safety First in Somerset.*" The disgruntled crustacean scowled and shook his head, causing his antennae to wildly bounce around. "It's just ridiculous!" he said. "I have a million things to do besides wandering around the city streets looking like a fool."

I lowered my voice and moved as close as I could, given the red legs jutting out from Andy's side. "We need to talk," I said. "Because I have a theory—"

I was interrupted by a little girl pulling at Andy's claws. "I want to dance with the funny lobster man," she pleaded with her mom.

Andy shot me an embarrassed look as he danced an awkward shuffle step with his young admirer.

We never got to talk, given that my booth got busy and Andy was always being pulled away to pose for a picture or to let a child pull on his arms. By the time Elizabeth came at one to take over for me, I had spotted the four Ackermans in line for lobster rolls.

After helping Elizabeth refill some of the sample bowls, I headed over there, and Jean waved and smiled. "Rue! So good to see you," she exclaimed.

Whitney gave me a soft smile. She was looking a bit better with a touch of color in her cheeks, and Matt gave me a wink. "Ah, the Lady of the Books," he said. "I hear you've been a lot of help to my family, Rue, and I do appreciate it."

I forced myself to nod and smile while Laila shoved half her lobster roll into my hand. "I'll never eat the whole thing," she said under her breath. "After seeing you-know-what on the computer, my appetite is gone."

We wandered past vendors selling jewelry, pottery, and more. Then we paused for a while to watch competitors building castles in lines of kiddie pools that had been filled with sand.

"I'm glad to see you out," I said, sidling up to Whitney.

"It feels good to be with people and to do something normal," she replied, sounding a bit more like herself.

"Mom, look over there!" said Kate. "There are those handmade purses you like to look at every year." And then she and Laila pulled their mom away.

"This was a good idea," said Matt. He dug his hands into his pockets. "I think she's doing better. But I just wish the foolish cops could solve this thing already."

"Oh, I have a feeling there will be an arrest real soon." I bit into my lobster roll, knowing the time had come to put my questions to him.

"You really think they have a suspect?" Matt's eyebrows shot straight up, and Jean looked at me, confused.

I took a deep breath. "Well, a possible motive in the killing has just now come to light." I lowered my tone. "It appears that Candace might have stumbled across some secrets someone wanted covered up." I looked straight into Matt's eyes. "Some pretty nasty secrets."

"Rue! What do you mean?" Jean gasped and grabbed my hand.

Matt's face had turned white.

"Financial fraud." I continued to stare at Matt. "And even worse than that. Candace, I suspect, had some information on how Jason died."

Jean's hand went to her mouth.

"It was someone close to Candace, I believe, so it must have been a shock." I gave Matt a death glare, and Jean's eyes darted between him and me as she tried to understand.

"You can't prove a thing! And neither can the cops," Matt sputtered as he got up into my face, causing many in the crowd to turn around and stare.

"Well, it's up to the evidence, not me, to tell the

story," I continued. "There are documents that indicate that you and David sold items from the store out of a warehouse for your personal financial gain. Before the store was yours, when you were just employees."

Jean gasped.

"And you had payments sent to another brother, who had no affiliation with Touchdowns and Home Runs," I continued.

"Who gave you the right to snoop in my brother's things?" he yelled.

By then, a crowd had gathered, including a stricken-looking trio of Whitney and her daughters.

"And when Jason learned your secrets, one of you made sure that he wouldn't tell by drowning him in Starling Lake."

"That kid had it coming!" shouted Matt, causing one of the castle builders to drop his plastic shovel. The others in the competition had gone still to listen breathlessly to the show.

"That kid had no business looking at the private stuff that David kept there in his house," said Matt, his face turning a bright red. "And then Candace started asking questions, and what could I do? I had to protect the reputation of the business that supports my brother's family and my own." He looked down at the ground. "What I meant to do was scare her with the knife so she'd let the matter drop. But then she got all self-righteous with me, and, well, I kind of snapped."

"Matt, did you kill Candace?" Jean asked him in a whisper.

Then Kate was beside us. "Did you kill Jason? Did my dad?"

Whitney let out a sob.

"I'm the one who did things right," he said in a hard voice. "My brother was the one who put us all in jeopardy by being careless with the papers and drowning that boy in the lake. All I ever tried to do was protect the family and cover up my brother's stupid acts. Then Candace, that do-gooder, would have gone and told everything she knew. And ruined my good name and yours." He pointed to a sobbing Whitney.

"Did he just confess to murder?" murmured someone in the crowd.

Then the growing knot of people parted to make way for a gigantic lobster lumbering toward us with a set of handcuffs in one claw and a handset in the other.

"I'm arresting him right now," he said into a handset. "Please send help ASAP. We have a lot of witnesses we'll need to interview."

CHAPTER NINETEEN

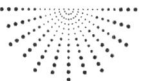

One week later, I hit "publish" on my website and met Kate at a rooftop bar on the beach to celebrate with champagne and oysters. It was a double celebration. Kate had just said yes to a marketing position not far outside of Boston.

"So I can come home on the weekends. I need to be close to family, for a while at least," she said.

"How is your mom?" I asked.

"Better every day but still really shaken up."

And it was no wonder. She had lost a daughter, plus she had figured out the man she had been married to for thirty years was not the man she knew. In the weeks before the murder as she had straightened up the house, she had peeked into old boxes that had been untouched for decades. And what she had seen was evidence of widespread fraud in the upper echelons of Touchdowns and Home Runs that had continued through the years. After they bought the business, the brothers had continued to operate outside the law, cheating on their taxes, affixing premium labels onto off-brand goods, making false claims against the competition, and much more.

Later, already numb with the loss of Candace, Whitney had searched desperately for signs of anything that could prove her husband hadn't been the criminal the documents had seemed to indicate. Plus, she didn't know how she could be impacted when all of the money he had left her was ill-gotten gains.

Then things began to spiral when she discovered hints that someone in the household might have been involved in Jason's death. Someone had printed stacks of Reddit threads about the subject and stuffed them into boxes. And she found several photos of the young man with his face x'ed out or angry words scrawled across his features.

Thus the need to purge and shred and sink into despair.

Andy had reported that the cops had begun hearing rumors about business fraud shortly after Candace died. That caused them to wonder if someone angry at the business had come after Candace in revenge.

Andy had explained that one such report had planted the idea in the minds of the cops that the guilty party might have plans to run and hide using the equipment that was now in vogue with preppers. One man had called in to say he had information regarding the Ackermans and a survival backpack. But when he came in to give a statement, it turned out that his story was not related to preparation for escape. The backpack full of goods was another ill-gotten item sold out of the warehouse in the early days. The product line had been sold by Touchdowns and Home Runs to the kinds of outdoors enthusiasts for whom the more remote the area the better when it came to hikes and camping out and getting close to nature.

Now I turned to Kate. "When do you start your job?" I asked, taking a sip of my champagne.

"Not for another three weeks," she told me. "First there is a trip—we're going to Alaska, me and Mom and Laila." She gave me a sheepish grin. "And you know, of course, that my mom has already packed her bags."

The family had come to learn that Whitney, in her desperation, had sought to consult with the former head attorney for the family business, who had also been a close confidant of David's. If anybody knew the truth behind the papers and the bits and pieces of information she had found, it would be Allen Ingalls. The only trouble was that Allen had retired to Alaska, and Whitney felt the sensitive conversation should be had face to face.

"Now there is no need for my mom to talk to Mr. Ingalls. Because Uncle Matt spilled out the ugly truth." Kate reached for an oyster. "But the three of us have a need for rest—and for glaciers and dogsledding and all of that good stuff."

"That sounds wonderful," I said. We made plans to get together in the next week to finalize the scholarship to honor Candace.

"My mom has all kinds of ideas," said Kate, "now that the truth is out and she can have some peace. Although to find out that it was Uncle Matt—what another massive blow. Life just keeps on swinging at us."

"I know how much you loved him, Kate. I just can't imagine how you feel," I said.

"Yeah, first we lose our father. Then our 'second father' turns out to be a monster. And our real father is a killer. Plus, now we have to deal with all the fallout from the business. Who knows what will happen with Touchdowns and Home Runs." She paused, lost in thought, as she slowly spun her almost-empty glass. "All the revelations really hit us hard, but it's been especially tough for Laila." She gave me a small smile. "But we have promised her a tour on snowmobiles when we get to Alaska. That was at the top of my sister's list."

I reached out to touch her arm. "You three have each other, and that will get you through," I said. "How are *you* doing, Kate?"

"I still can't wrap my brain around the fact that Candace won't come walking through the door any minute now. I mean, she was here and then she wasn't." She stared down at the table. "The last thing that I said to her was that she was a slob, that she should get her act together and figure out her life. All of those ugly words kept running through my brain on a constant loop after she was killed. And in some ways, Ms. Collier, she was the best of all of us. I wish I'd told her that."

"Oh, I imagine that she knew how you really felt. But that's the way it is when we lose someone that we love. We are always thinking we will have more time."

"Which is why I wrote these letters to all of my best friends and told them everything I wanted them to know. I could be gone tomorrow, or they could be gone. So we should say all the things today that we want to say."

I looked up at the night sky. "I don't see your lion up there in the stars."

"But I like to think he's up there watching over me even when I can't pick him out in the sky. My father always told me the world is full of wonders the human eye can't see; we just have to believe." She stared into her drink. "Not that David Ackerman was some great source of wisdom I want to emulate. But sometimes he spoke the truth, and there might come a day when I can think of him and not just sob with fury. Or at least I hope there will." Her voice grew very soft. "I can't reconcile the man I knew with that kind of evil." She closed her eyes against the thought. "It still just doesn't fit."

Matt had told the police that David was the brother most determined to flaunt any kind of ethics on the way to greater profits. As the older, more cautious brother, Matt became the one to clean up the messes, which left him increasingly livid with his brother through the years. I guessed that explained the photos I had seen with an angry Matt lurking in the background of happy family moments.

Matt had been incensed when David had tasked Jason with writing up the history of the company. Too much in the history of Touchdowns and Home Runs was better left alone, but David's ambition had always been tainted by a streak of carelessness. Matt, as an example, had told David about a million times to get rid of any evidence that might have gotten left around the house or office for anyone to find. When Jason grew suspicious after finding incriminating papers in the office files, Matt had gone ballistic. Then came the romance between Kate and Jason, which meant that Jason had begun spending time in David's home, where the real evidence of fraud was kept.

And then when David had confessed to the murder, Matt had driven to Somerset Harbor to coach his brother on how to avoid getting caught—the same as he had done with David's lesser crimes. The lion statue had been an extravagant gift from David to his young protégé, whom he hoped would become an integral part of the company after his graduation. After drowning Jason, he had stuffed the statue in his pocket, thinking he could get tens of thousands of dollars for it rather than just leaving it tucked inside the backpack. But Matt had understood the missing statue could be linked to the crime, and he had insisted that his brother hide the lion away in his home office. Where it had remained, tucked into a box in the back of a closet, until Candace pulled it out.

David's heart attack had come the same year as the drowning. I found myself wondering if the stress had played a role.

When I looked up from my musings, Kate was watching me intently.

"I know you love your books," she said. "But have

you ever thought of being a detective? You were kind of badass at the Lobster Fest with my Uncle Matt."

I waved the thought away. "Too dangerous for me. I'll leave that to the cops."

Kate burst into giggles. "And to the giant lobsters that roam the streets downtown, always at the ready to fight crime."

"That was my buddy, Andy, who can never catch a break," I said with a grin. "It turns out the lobster suit was the chief's idea of giving him a day off from the case."

Kate let out a laugh. "That was some day off!"

"Now he can never order lobster without some smart remark from me," I said with a smile.

Kate lifted a brow. "Sir, would you like your lobster fried or boiled or would you prefer it served with pepper spray and handcuffs?"

"Insert your own joke," I said. "I should come up with a list."

Kate gave me a shy smile. "Thank you for tonight," she told me. "I never thought I'd laugh again." She lifted her glass. "Here's to laughter and to friends," she said.

I held up my glass, and the stars seemed to wink to echo her toast.

# # #

Thank you for reading! Want to help out?

Reviews are crucial for independent authors like me, so if you enjoyed my book, **please consider leaving a review today**.

Thank you!

Penny Brooke

ABOUT THE AUTHOR

Penny Brooke has been reading mysteries for as long as she can remember. When not penning her own stories, she enjoys spending time outdoors with her husband, crocheting, and cozying up with her pups and a good novel. To find out more about her books, visit www.pennybrooke.com

Made in the USA
Las Vegas, NV
15 July 2023

74766052R10089